A CASE OF GRAVE DANGER

Books by Sophie Cleverly

The Violet Veil Mysteries in reading order

A CASE OF GRAVE DANGER

The Scarlet and Ivy series in reading order

THE LOST TWIN

THE WHISPERS IN THE WALLS

THE DANCE IN THE DARK

THE LIGHTS UNDER THE LAKE

THE CURSE IN THE CANDLELIGHT

THE LAST SECRET

SOPHIE CLEVERLY

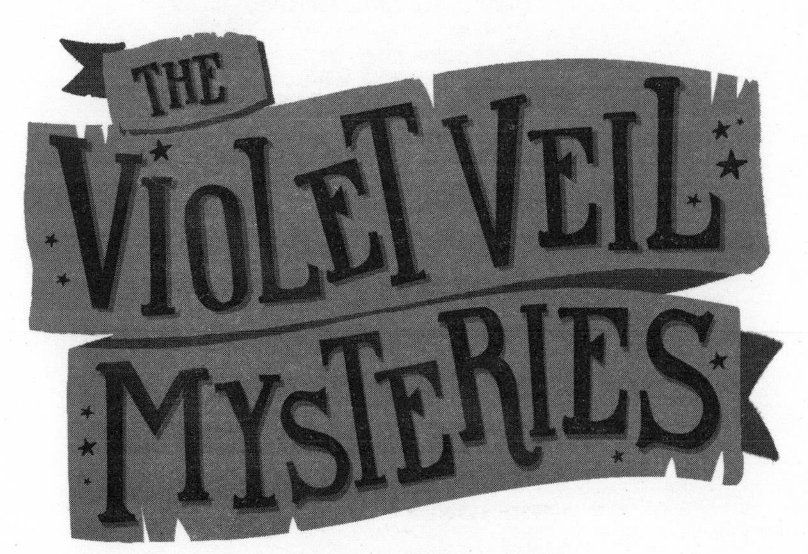

A CASE OF GRAVE DANGER

HarperCollins *Children's Books*

First published in Great Britain by
HarperCollins *Children's Books* in 2021

HarperCollins Children's Books is a division of HarperCollins*Publishers* Ltd
HarperCollins*Publishers*
1 London Bridge Street
London SE1 9GF

www.harpercollins.co.uk

HarperCollins*Publishers*
1st Floor, Watermarque Building, Ringsend Road Dublin 4, Ireland

1

ISBN 978-0-00-829735-0

Sophie Cleverly and Hannah Peck assert the moral right to be identified
as the author and illustrator of the work respectively.

Typeset in Plantin 11/18 pt
Printed and bound in England by CPI Group (UK) Ltd, Croydon CR0 4YY

A CIP catalogue record for this title is available from the British Library.

MIX
Paper from
responsible sources
FSC™ C007454

This book is produced from independently certified FSC™ paper
to ensure responsible forest management.

For more information visit: www.harpercollins.co.uk/green

For Lyanna – I love you more than all the stars in the sky

Chapter One

I was born in the mortuary. Topsy-turvy, I know, but that's the truth of it. My mother said the slab was cold and hard, but that she was in no fit state to quarrel at the time.

They named me Violet, for the flower – the twin to my mother's name, Iris. I think they were hoping I would be a Shrinking Violet, modest and shy, but it was soon apparent that I was not.

My middle name is Victoria, after the queen. They said she was in mourning for her husband these days, roaming the palace dressed only in black. I didn't see anything unusual about that. Father had clothed us in dark and sombre colours for as long as I could remember. 'We're always in mourning for someone,' he'd say.

Being on the edge of life and death was a funny thing. Sometimes, out among the graves, I could sense the dead. It was just a feeling – an echo of emotion, a scattering of words. It was just a part of me, and I had grown used to it – grown used to keeping quiet about it too, because all I got were strange looks and shushes from grown-ups if I were to mention it.

Often the dead didn't have much to say. But I was soon to encounter a dead person who had a *lot* more to say than usual.

The day of the miracle, I had recently turned thirteen years old, and I was out collecting apples in the cemetery. I took a bite of one and it was as crisp as the autumn air. My black greyhound, Bones, ran circles around my feet, sniffing the ground with his long nose.

Bones was a fairly recent addition to the family. I had found him wandering amongst the headstones. As soon as he'd spotted me, he wouldn't leave me alone. He wore no collar and looked skinny – but then all greyhounds do.

I named him Bones, because growing up as the daughter of an undertaker and living, as we did, beside a graveyard, it just seemed fitting. I fed him scraps and begged Mother to let me keep him. She said no. So I asked Father, who said maybe. Mother finally gave in and said I could have him, but all the same, she made Bones sleep outside.

For two weeks, he slept just beyond our back wall, curled at the foot of a stone cross. By the third week, Mother took pity on him and let him sleep in the back garden. It was only a few days more before he was in the house, and often on my bed.

Now he was my constant companion – at least when he wasn't distracted by doggy things such as chasing squirrels and chewing shoes.

That day, when my skirts were full of the ripe fruit, I dashed back through the graves and into the parlour – the funeral parlour, that is – leaving Bones rolling in the grass. The breeze whipped my long dark hair across my eyes.

Father was sweeping up when I got in. 'Honestly, Violet, can't you use the back door to the house? What if there had been someone in here?'

'Someone?' I chuckled. 'Your guests are usually a little too dead to notice, aren't they, Father!'

He huffed at me and shook the broom out of the open door. I turned to see Bones trying to get a mouthful of broom before Father tugged it back. 'And what about the family members? They could be visiting the deceased.'

'We don't have any visitors. Not today. I know the arrangements. I do pay attention *sometimes*, you know.'

'Really? You surprise me.' He tousled my hair affectionately and then mopped his brow. 'What are you going to do with all those apples?' he asked, but he turned away and I could tell he was no longer paying attention. In the past he would have played with me, juggled the apples, told me some little story about how fruit was somehow a metaphor for life – but he always seemed rather distracted these days.

I looked around the room. My arms were aching with the weight of my skirts, and I suddenly realised I wouldn't be able to hold on to them much longer, but neither did I want to spill the apples all over the floor.

Aha! There was a coffin on the dais, freshly varnished and upholstered but currently empty. Perfect. I lifted the front of my dress and tipped them all in.

It made quite a racket, as you can probably imagine. *That* got his attention.

'VIOLET!' he shouted, spinning round. 'Good heavens, girl, whatever do you think you're doing?'

I grinned at him. 'I just needed somewhere to put them down for a moment. Don't worry! I'll have them out of here before you can spit.'

'I do not. Wish. To spit,' he replied.

I realised it was time for a hasty exit. So, with Bones trailing behind me, I scooped up an armful of the red apples and headed through the door into the house.

Mother was in the kitchen, darning some of Thomas's socks by the fire.

'Apples!' I called cheerily.

She looked up and smiled, her bright eyes lighting the room. 'More apples? I'll be making a pie or three, then. Add them to the basket in the larder.'

I did as she said. When I returned, she spoke again. 'You know, my dear old mother used to say that an orchard in a graveyard could only grow bones. How wrong she was!' She pulled a finished sock from her darning mushroom and tossed it aside. 'Though we do seem to be overburdened with apples.' She looked down at the dog. 'I'm sure this one would prefer a beef bone.'

Bones pricked up his ears and sat wagging his tail, perhaps hoping Mother might actually have one somewhere about her person.

'You could make a fine bone broth with one,' I said.

My brother, Thomas, came in just then, his black trousers scuffed at the knees with dirt and grass stains. 'Yeeuch!' he exclaimed, throwing his leather football to the floor. 'Who wants nasty old bone broth?'

Mother reached up and gave him a gentle clip on the ear– he was only six years old, and not yet as tall as me. He was at home for a few weeks after his school had been flooded. I still thought it unfair that he was seven years younger than me, but got to go to school when I didn't. But then I was a girl and he was a boy and that was just how it was.

'You'll eat what you're given and be thankful, whether it's broth or five apple pies. We have to make do these days. And look at the state of your trousers!' Mother was forever having to fix and alter our clothes, whether it was for repairs or to try and keep up with the latest fashions.

Thomas dragged a chair out from under the table, scraping the legs on the floor. Then he sat down heavily on it and ruffled a hand through his dark hair. A few blades of grass fell out. Bones ran over and sniffed them while Mother rolled her eyes at the sight.

I was about to return for more apples (after all, Father would not be pleased if I left them where they were) when Thomas spoke again.

'Mother,' he said, 'who's to be buried in plot two hundred and thirty-nine?'

Bones looked up at him, his eyes like small galaxies.

Mother put down the darning mushroom and stared at the wall for a moment in thought. 'Is that one of the new ones? It's just been dug out?'

'Yes,' he replied solemnly.

'A young man, I think. He came in this morning. No relatives have come forward for him, poor thing. But your father will see to it that he gets a good burial. He always does. Even though it isn't very good for business.'

I shivered a little, and took hold of a chair-back to steady myself. I remembered the young man she was talking about from earlier. He was fairly tall and pale, with blond hair (a little on the long side). He couldn't have been much older than me – sixteen, perhaps? I'd sat with him for some time, just talking to him quietly – even the dead need company, though I never heard much back from them when they had recently passed. It was as though they hadn't settled in yet.

'Why do you ask, Thomas?' I said.

He looked up at me. 'I just wondered. There's been a few in a row. What if it was murder?' He made a horrified face. *'Murder most foul?'*

Mother narrowed her eyebrows at him, her favourite look of disapproval. 'Murders? What nonsense. You've got a vivid imagination, my boy. Have you been reading those Penny Dreadfuls again? They are *not* suitable reading material for a boy of your age.'

Thomas stuck his tongue out, and I covered my mouth with one hand to suppress a giggle.

Mother tutted at him. 'Your imagination is running away with you,' she continued. 'There have just been some nasty accidents, that's all.' She went back to her darning.

Bones padded round the table and sat by my feet. I stared into his soulful eyes and, not for the first time, wondered what he was thinking. He had a strange sense for these things, as did I. My skin was beginning to tingle, and I wondered if there was something to Thomas's bizarre theory. There *had* been an unusual amount of men in their prime in the past couple of weeks – three or four, I thought. And now this boy. I wondered what could have happened to him. Surely it couldn't be murder – Father would have noticed.

'Violet!' Father was calling me from the funeral parlour. *Oops.* He was certainly angry now. When I was sure that Mother wasn't looking, I pulled a grotesque face at Thomas and then headed back down the corridor.

'Violet,' he repeated when I entered the room, followed by Bones. 'Something's missing.'

'What?' I asked. I noticed that he had removed most of the apples already, and began to wonder if the coffin would be the one for the blond boy.

'One of the files.'

He gestured for me to follow him into the shop at the front of the house (not really a shop in the strictest sense of the word, of course – but death was our business, and money was exchanged here). The shop was filled with gloomy oak furniture – chairs, a desk, bookshelves and row after row of huge filing cabinets that contained all the information about those who were now resident in the cemetery. It was all so dark that I wondered how other people could stand to be in there for any length of time, especially when they had just lost a loved one. Father said it was respectful.

Thankfully, that day the autumn sun was bright and spilled in through the gaps in the heavy curtains. A carriage rattled past outside and a few flecks of dirt splattered on to the glass.

'It was here,' said Father. I blinked, my eyes adjusting to the light, and turned to where he was standing. He pointed into one of the drawers in the cabinet.

I walked over and took a look at a row of files. Bones sniffed them curiously. 'I don't see anything.'

'Precisely! It's missing!' He wriggled two of the files this way and that with his fingertips. 'There should be a file here, the one for the boy who came in early this morning.'

I looked at the names written on the top of the paper in my father's neat hand. All of them read the same: *John Doe*. 'The blond boy?'

'Yes. Did you take it, perhaps?' He gave me a stern look, and I began to feel a little uneasy. I certainly hadn't taken it, but under his gaze I felt guilty, as though I *had* done something. Did he suspect me because he'd seen me talking to the boy as he'd lain there?

I squirmed. 'No, Father. I haven't seen the file at all.'

He wrinkled his brow. 'Well, do you have any idea who might have done?'

I thought about it. 'Thomas, perhaps? He was asking about the boy just now. He seems to have some theory about murder, but Mother said he's just been reading too much nonsense.'

There was a moment of silence as Father stared at the wall, and then pushed his spectacles higher up his nose. 'Thomas,' he repeated. 'Of course, I should ask Thomas as well.' He walked back out of the shop again, in the direction of the house.

I went over to the window and brushed a few cobwebs away. We kept rows of flowers there, tastefully arranged in vases to show what manner of establishment we were. The sign above the door read

EDGAR D. VEIL AND SONS LTD. UNDERTAKERS.

The Edgar that it referred to was my grandfather, now

five years dead, and my father Edgar Junior was his only remaining son. I'd told Father that he ought to change it to *Edgar Veil and Son and Daughter Ltd*, but he had only laughed and ruffled my hair.

I had been serious, though. Why shouldn't I be recognised as part of the family business just because I was a girl? I did a lot more work than Thomas did.

Well, except for when I was picking apples instead.

The glass in the shop window was rippled with age, but you could still see through it. Now, as I glanced up, I could see a woman on the outside, looking in at the porcelain flowers.

A mourner, I thought. *A widow in black. She must be here to arrange a funeral.*

Yet there was something strange about her. I couldn't see her eyes behind the waterfall of black lace and pale hair that cascaded past her shoulders, yet I felt for sure they were now staring straight at me.

Bones began to growl softly, a low rumbling in his throat.

'Shh, boy,' I said. 'Don't scare the customers.'

I thought I ought to go out and greet her, but then the woman quickly turned her head and darted across the street, hitching up her skirts as she went.

I frowned. Why had she looked so furtive? But before I could think anything more of it, I heard raised voices coming from the house.

'I did *not* take your silly file!'

'Thomas! Don't you dare talk that way to your father!'

My family could be rather a nightmare at times. Was it any wonder that I often preferred the company of the dead? At least they seldom argued.

With a sigh, I headed back to the kitchen.

⋆ ⋆ ⋆

That evening, after supper, Father lit the gas lamp and we all sat round the fire in the parlour. I tried to read my book, Mary Shelley's *Frankenstein*, but I couldn't concentrate and my eyes kept slipping away from it. It was dark outside, and I could hear the rain falling over the crackle of the fire. Bones was sleeping on the rug, pawing at imaginary rats in his dreams.

Thomas wasn't talking to Father after their squabble earlier. He sat in the corner of the room, painting wooden soldiers with a grim expression on his face. Occasionally I heard him mutter something to himself under his breath about not being a thief.

I began to think again about the missing file as I stared into the flames. Maybe Father had just misplaced it, but was there a chance that someone had taken it? Who would want to steal records on a boy that nobody knew?

If they'd known who he was, and that he was dead, they would have come to claim him, wouldn't they? Unless Thomas was right, and someone *had* murdered the blond boy. I felt a tingle of a shiver run down my spine.

We'd had murder victims in before, of course. Not many, but enough. Yet the blond boy, who now lay in his apple-free coffin, seemed different somehow.

Tap.

'What was that?' asked Thomas.

I'd heard it too. I looked to the window. Only darkness.

Bones's ears pricked up, and suddenly he was on his feet, staring in the direction of the sound.

'Perhaps it was the tree outside,' said Father, tapping the bowl of his pipe out into the ashtray. 'I've been meaning to ask the groundskeeper to cut it back. The branches are getting too near the house.'

'It didn't come from upstairs,' Thomas insisted. 'It came from out *there*.' He pointed to the front window.

'Probably only the rain, my dear,' said Mother. 'Come along now, Thomas, it's past your bedtime.' She stood up and shepherded my little brother out of the room, despite his protests.

Father simply shrugged and went back to reading his newspaper.

But I hadn't looked away from the window. Because I had seen something that the others had not.

A flash of white eyes in the darkness, and a shadow disappearing into the night.

Chapter Two

I couldn't sleep that night, though goodness knows I tried. My down quilt felt hot and heavy, and no matter which way I turned I couldn't get comfortable. I knew, though, that wasn't the real reason I couldn't sleep. It was because of the face I'd seen at the window.

The grandfather clock downstairs was chiming an hour past my bedtime, but my eyes hadn't closed. I couldn't stop thinking about what I'd seen. Someone had been out there, looking in on us. What if they had been a grave robber or a vandal? I wouldn't forgive myself if something happened.

Why I hadn't told my father about what I'd seen, I don't know. Perhaps I thought he wouldn't listen, given how preoccupied he seemed at the moment. But I hadn't said a word, and now if anything *did* happen, I'd be responsible.

And it was after that thought that I heard a noise downstairs.

Bones, who had been sleeping on my bed (which, needless to say, he was not supposed to do), woke up and began growling softly. He hopped down, padded over to the door and started to paw at the floorboards.

I had to go and look.

It was a ridiculous idea, and I tried to talk myself out of it. What could I possibly do if I confronted a dangerous villain? Nothing but call for help, and by then it could be too late. If they ran, I could chase them, I supposed, but it was night-time and the autumn sky was black as ink.

I wasn't scared of being in a graveyard – how could I be, when I had been raised here? In the daylight, when the sun was shining and the poppies and daisies would gently blow in the breeze, it was beautiful. At night, things where different. The moon wouldn't be enough light to see by, and a candle would be extinguished by the rain. I was fairly certain I had nothing to fear from the dead, but the living were another matter altogether.

More noises came to my ears: shuffling and banging.

Bones's tail went upright like an exclamation mark. His eyes met mine, and I nodded at him. I felt my courage building, knowing that he was by my side. He could probably give anyone he didn't like the look of a good bite.

I found myself throwing off the covers and climbing out of bed. I pulled open the door as quietly as I could and tiptoed down the landing. I could hear Mother snoring gently and the ever-present rain on the rooftops.

I slipped silently down the stairs, Bones padding ahead of me – his footsteps remarkably quiet for a large dog. He went straight for the funeral parlour, and started barking. In trepidation, I followed. I felt something was wrong immediately, but it took a few moments for me to realise what it was.

I peered around the dark room, at outlines in the gloom of shelves and coffins and urns. I stepped further inside, and I could see the edge of the coffin on the dais, the sharp angles of the cheap wood, and my eyes swept past it to the tiled floor.

And then I looked again.

The coffin was empty.

Only hours ago, the blond boy had been lying in it. It was the same coffin, that much was certain. It still smelled faintly of apples.

Thoughts raced through my head.

It's a grave robber. Or a murderer has come back to steal the body. Or . . . I gulped, thinking of Frankenstein's creation in the novel as it shuddered to life.

Bones wobbled around the room, sniffing everything. I tried to contain my panic, told myself I should just go back to bed. But in a flash, Bones was racing out of the door, heading for the back of the house.

I didn't know why, but I felt I had to follow. It took all my strength to put one foot in front of the other, but I did it. I felt a cold breeze on my skin, and heard the sound of falling rain grow louder.

Now Bones batted at the back door, whining. It was open a crack. Someone had come inside.

Or gone out.

After a deep breath, I pulled the door back a little and peered through. I could see nothing but rain. *A lantern*, I thought. That was what I needed. Father often kept one by the back door.

I snuck into the tiny cloakroom by the porch and pulled out a black overcoat that was a little too big for me, buttoning it on over my nightgown. Soft leather boots that were now old and battered went on over my feet – they felt odd without any stockings.

The glass lantern was on a hook next to the door, almost too high for me to reach, but I managed it on tiptoes. There was a white candle stub inside, so I found a box of matches and lit it. Then I took a deep breath. It was time for a very unwise decision.

I stepped outside.

The rain fell around me in waves, immediately sticking strands of my hair to my forehead. Gooseflesh rose on my legs in seconds as the wind bit into them. The light from the lantern illuminated only a mere few feet in front of my eyes. Bones quivered in the cold, before striding ahead into the dark.

There were fresh footprints in the mud, leading away from the house. Human footprints. Footprints that were just a little larger than mine.

Definitely an unwise decision.

As I went through our back gate, the footprints disappeared as the grass of the cemetery took over.

I began to walk through the graves. I knew them well. I passed John Beckington and steadied myself on the headstone. I passed Annie Arkwright and Mr and Mrs Jones and Jeremiah Heap. I stopped for breath by the O'Neill family crypt and leaned against the cold wall. The vast tomb gave a little shelter, at least.

If I listened hard enough, I could hear their whispers.

Keep going.

You're close.

They sensed something that I could not. So far I had seen nothing but the faint grey shadows of the ghosts, which shifted and changed like wisps of fog. I had heard no movement in the grass or trees, no sounds of footsteps or heavy breathing. But it was so dark and so loud out there that I began to wonder if I wasn't being totally foolish. Perhaps I had just imagined the footprints, the way they looked. Perhaps they had belonged to Thomas from earlier in the day, and I just hadn't noticed them before.

The only way I would know if someone was there was if they jumped out at me, and that wasn't an idea I relished. Bones was still moving forward, as if he had caught a scent.

I shivered. I was sure to catch a chill in this weather. 'Who's there?' I whispered, blinking through the rain at the iron clouds and the few stars that dappled the empty space between. I wondered if I might hear a ghostly answer, but whatever I sensed from the dead, it was never an answer to my burning questions.

It was time to move on – I needed to keep going. I could see Bones running on ahead, investigating the graves as he passed. I decided I would loop back on myself once I got to the far hedgerow (I longed for my bed already), but I soon realised I was getting nearer to the spot where the blond boy was to be buried.

Bones stopped at the graveside, where the freshly dug hole gaped like the mouth of Hell. Then I really could hear something. A moaning sound that seemed as though it were coming from the grave.

I was near paralysed with fear. Bones hung close to my leg, and I felt his skin rumbling as he growled.

Slowly, I dangled the lantern and peered in.

The grave was empty. Nothing but a muddy hole, rapidly filling with rainwater.

The sound reached my ears this time. It was definitely someone moaning. I bit my lip so hard that I could taste blood.

'H-hello?' I called into the night. 'Is someone there?' I blinked in the rain, in the flickering glow of the candlelight.

Something moved behind one of the gravestones. A shadow, shuffling, ungainly.

Watch out, one of the ghostly voices whispered on the breeze.

I gasped, and Bones barked into the wind. The shadow

moved nearer, pushing through the grass. I stayed frozen, held out the lantern like a shield. I wasn't sure if I wanted to see what was approaching, but I had no choice.

A figure lurched into the light, and I caught a strangled breath in my throat.

There, standing before me, was the blond boy. The boy who was supposed to be dead.

I screamed.

Chapter Three

'You're ALIVE!' I gasped.

Alive, the deathly voices around me echoed in whispers. *Not one of us*. This would be the talk of the graveyard now.

The blond boy was dressed in funeral finery, the best that could be put together for a pauper from the tailor's cast-offs, but even so – his face was as pale as the moon above us, a sliver of it peeking through the dark clouds. He was soaked with rain, dishevelled and muddy, his hair sticking up at strange angles. His skin was ashen, his eyes sunken and hollow, blinking in the light.

I finally caught my breath again. 'Are you all right?'

The boy stumbled towards me, and I jerked backwards. Bones barked again, a warning.

The boy opened his mouth, as if not quite sure how it worked. He rubbed a hand against the back of his head. 'Where . . . am I?' he asked, the words coming slowly like they were rising up through treacle.

I shushed Bones and held on to his collar. 'You're in the graveyard,' I said. 'Um, well, Seven Gates Cemetery, to be precise.' I realised that I was going to have to step a little nearer, but my legs were fighting against me. I ignored them and moved closer to the boy so he could hear me.

'Are you a ghost? Am I . . . dead?' the blond boy asked, his dark eyes wide with terror.

I paused, a little taken aback by his humanity. Perhaps he wasn't some terrifying creature of the night after all.

'I'm certainly not a ghost!' I said. 'Ghosts are more . . .' I looked down at myself. 'See-through. And *you* certainly don't *look* dead,' I admitted. 'In fact, you seem rather upright.'

The boy suddenly stumbled sideways, falling into the mud beside the grave. Bones pulled away from me and began to lick his face.

'*Violet! Violet!* Are you there?'

It was Father! I had never been so thankful in my entire life. *'Father!* Come quick, please!'

He dashed through the darkness towards me, his hand shielding his eyes. 'What on earth . . .' he shouted as the water drummed on the stones around us. Bones pressed a wet nose against his trousers. My father was wearing nightclothes under an overcoat, like myself.

I watched as Father slowly took in the sight before him – the pouring rain, his daughter looking like a drowned rat, and the blond boy slumped against a stone cross, chest heaving with the breath of life.

'Oh my . . .' Father said, as though hardly able to believe his own eyes. He looked at me desperately. 'What's going on here?'

'I don't know!' I said breathlessly. 'I heard a noise, so I went downstairs, and I found his coffin empty! The door was open, and there were footprints . . .'

Father pulled me into his arms. There was a brief moment of warmth and shelter, before he released me. 'You should have fetched me immediately! There could have been grave robbers about!' His words were cut short as he looked at the boy again. I didn't know how Father could see a thing – his spectacles were steamed up and splattered with rain. 'How could this have happened?' His face had gone as pale as the boy's.

The boy shook his head as if trying to regain his senses, and shivered in the cold. He looked up at us, and finally spoke again. 'W-what's . . . happened to me?'

* * *

The blond boy was dead. He *had* been dead. Hadn't he? He'd been sent to us to be buried – I'd seen it with my own two eyes. And yet, whatever he had been, he was very much alive now and firmly back in the land of the living.

Father held a shaking hand out to the boy. The boy took it, but it took several attempts to lift him up – his weakened legs kept buckling beneath him. When he was finally standing, he seemed to be capable of staying up. I wanted to take his hand so badly, to give him comfort in any way that I could, but Mother's voice in the back of my head whispered that it would be improper.

He moaned again, and tried to bat the light away.

'He's delirious,' Father said.

I gulped. 'It's all right,' I said to the boy, trying my best to soothe his quick breaths. 'Please, stay calm. We need to get you inside. Can you walk?'

'I think so,' he said, but his voice was barely a whisper, and I wasn't sure whether I'd truly heard or only seen his lips move.

Father tentatively put his hands on the boy's shoulders. 'I'll run for Doctor Lane. Violet will help you back to the house, if you can make it.'

The boy nodded again, silently, and I couldn't help but shudder. I knew he was alive, but at the same time still felt as though he were a dead man walking. Like Frankenstein's monster.

In the lamplight, I could see that he was covered with mud and damp grass. Bones gently licked him.

Then Father was running, and Bones shot away after him with a sudden burst of greyhound speed. They darted through the headstones like minnow through a stream – they knew them as well as I did.

The blond boy staggered again, and I ducked underneath his arm to try to bear him up. *To heck with improper*, I thought. *He needs me*. And I couldn't keep calling him 'the blond boy'. 'What's your name, master?' I asked.

'Oliver,' he replied, and then he began coughing violently.

When the coughing subsided, I spoke again. 'Can you walk? We'll need to get you back to the house. You'll catch your de—' I stopped myself. 'Sorry.'

He didn't seem to notice my *faux pas*. He began to stumble forward, and together we walked back through the rain-washed graveyard, the mud and sodden grass threatening to pull our shoes from our feet. I tried to steer him around the graves, but at one point he tripped on Nathaniel Partridge's broken headstone and nearly brought us both down.

It seemed like it took an age, the two of us walking in silence under the black sky. The ghosts' voices were mere tingling whispers now – I fancied they were talking amongst themselves, not to me, about the evening's excitement. The barrier between living and dead was a hard one to cross, like shouting underwater.

As the clouds began to melt away, I glimpsed stars beginning to twinkle. 'Not long now,' I kept saying. 'Nearly there.' Eventually it was true, and we were outside the back door.

It was wide open – Father must have run through the house.

The boy – Oliver – stopped and leaned against the wall, his breathing still rapid. One of his hands clutched his stomach, the other his head. I quickly reached inside the door and stretched to hang up the lantern on the hook, so that I had both hands free.

'Please . . . Master Oliver,' I said. 'You've got to get inside.'

He looked at me, and I was suddenly struck by his eyes, which were – for all their sunkenness – a deep, dark brown like a warm cup of cocoa. So different from my own, which were storm grey.

'I . . .' he paused. 'I don't want to tread mud inside your house, miss.'

And then he fainted.

Chapter Four

When Oliver's eyes finally blinked back open, he looked rather surprised to see myself, my father, my mother (who had been awoken by all the commotion), Doctor Lane and Bones the dog all staring down at him. He tried to speak, but it rapidly dissolved into coughing.

'Don't talk for a little while, son,' said the doctor, his voice deep and booming. 'Your throat is raw.'

Oliver nodded, or at least attempted a nod, but it was clearly rather difficult as he was lying down.

Doctor Lane leaned closer and held a light up to the boy's eyes. 'Do you remember what happened to you?'

A short, sharp shake of the head.

'But you remember who you are?'

'My name's Oliver,' came the whispered reply, and that was all he could say.

We'd got him to the nearest bed, which happened to be mine since Thomas was still fast asleep. Needless to say, my cream quilt was no longer looking creamy, and was instead blemished with mud and grass. Bones had decided to curl up on the end of the bedspread, contributing to the mess.

I'd taken a chair next to the bed. Oliver was staring up at me. His lips were dry and cracked as he mouthed something.

'Water!' I said. 'He needs water!'

I looked at Mother, who was tightly gripping a bottle of smelling salts in a worried fashion. 'Oh, yes,' she replied. 'I'll get some.' She hurried out of the room.

Doctor Lane yawned and began to fold up his stethoscope. 'Will you be able to look after this young man until tomorrow? He might be a little in shock, but the rest of him, miraculously, seems to be in order. His heartbeat is strong and his breathing is returning to normal.'

'Hmm, all right,' Father said. He was still soaked

through and muddy, as was I. 'He can rest here,' he said wearily. 'Let me get your coat.'

Doctor Lane gathered up his leather bag and headed out of the door, followed by Father. Bones stayed at the boy's feet. He liked him, I could tell.

I reached out and gently took Oliver's hand. It was freezing. He winced a little, but remained silent. I thought he would shut his eyes, yet they stayed wide open, and he appeared to be focusing on the light of the lamp.

Lying there so pale, with his eyes unblinking, he looked almost like the corpse we'd believed him to be to start with. Yet his chest rose and fell, and a little colour was slowly returning to his complexion.

I knew well that death was the end of everyone's story. Or at least it *should* be. But this boy – Oliver – he was somehow still here. His story hadn't ended. This wasn't the faint, whispery epilogue from the ghosts that sometimes tickled the edge of my hearing. He was real, and here, and alive. If life were a book, he had been given a sequel. Was it a misunderstanding or a miracle?

Mother returned to the room then, with the water, interrupting my musings. It amused me to see that she had put it into an old baby feeding bottle – the round glass kind with a rubber tube out of the top. I could soon see why. She propped it up next to Oliver in the bed, and he sipped it gratefully. His breathing quickened as he gulped down the water.

'Careful now,' said my mother, patting his damp forehead gently. 'We don't want you to choke.'

'We certainly don't,' I agreed.

Mother was giving me a questioning look. I looked down and realised I was still holding on to Oliver's hand. I let go as discreetly as I could.

She shook her head at me. 'Come along, Violet. We'll get you a change of nightdress and you can sleep in our bed until morning. Your father's going to stay up. He says he won't be able to sleep again after all this rigmarole.'

Well, that was one way of putting it.

Better than *'all this mess where the boy we thought was dead was in fact alive and wandering the cemetery in the dark of night'*.

I stood up and followed Mother out of the room. But I risked one last glance back at Oliver, the dog still resting at the end of his feet, guarding him.

I could have sworn I saw the edges of his lips curl into a weak smile.

★ ★ ★

The next day (or I suppose later the same day, for I'd been awake most of the night), as the sun pushed through the rainclouds and streamed in through the window, my first thoughts were of Oliver. Or admittedly, that the whole thing had been a nightmare. It was only as I rubbed my eyes and saw my parents' eiderdown and heavy furniture that I realised it had been real.

Mother had already risen and neatly made her side of the bed. I swung my legs off the side. Even though I'd scrubbed most of the mud off in the washbasin, there was still some remaining on my skin. I stood up and peered in the mirror – I looked like someone who'd been trawling through a graveyard in the rain. No surprises there.

I sneaked a glance into my room as I walked past. Oliver was sitting up in the bed, a breakfast tray on his lap, Bones still happily snoozing by his feet. The boy smiled at me weakly. I blinked and smiled back, before remembering I was still only wearing a nightgown. It might've escaped people's notice last night, but I knew I'd be in big trouble if I didn't get dressed properly. The only problem was that all of my clothes were in my bedroom. Hmm.

I walked on. 'Mother!' I shouted down the stairs.

'Don't shout, Violet!' she shouted back. 'It's unladylike!'

'Can you fetch my clothes for me?' I asked. 'My room's occupied.'

I heard a sigh, followed by, 'Of course, darling.'

Until a few years ago, we'd had servants in the house

who would have done that sort of thing for us – Thomas and I had had a nanny and then two governesses, first Miss Stone and then Mrs Barker – but one by one they had all left our service. Costs had to be cut, according to Father, because everyone was having to tighten their belts these days. I was devastated when our housekeeper had left – her name had been Mrs Keaton and she was the warmest and friendliest of people. She'd always give me sugar cubes as a treat when Mother wasn't looking.

We still had one servant remaining, though – Maddy. Maddy lived in one of the two attic rooms at the top of the stairs. She was a housemaid, and it was her job to light the fires in the morning, to clean and polish, and to change the beds. She would usually take on ladies' maid duties, too, helping us wash and dress. She'd been away the past few days; Father had allowed her to have her yearly week of time off to visit her family in Yorkshire.

This meant that Mother was doing a lot more than she was used to. As she helped me into my dress that morning, she kept sighing and muttering about how there weren't sufficient hours in the day. It was almost enough to make me feel bad for rescuing Oliver and giving her more to worry about.

Almost.

Mother cooked us a breakfast of slivers of bacon and

eggs with (nearly) fresh bread. It was a struggle to finish it; my stomach was churning. I supposed the events of last night hadn't been good for me. I was still awfully worried about Oliver. Exactly why, I couldn't say. I barely knew him. I'd spent more time with him 'dead' than alive.

That was a thought. I looked up from my plate at Father, who was polishing his shoes opposite me. The question had been plaguing me all night. 'Was Oliver really dead, Father?'

His mouth twisted as he considered it. 'I don't think so. Doctor Lane said he was unconscious. There's a wound on the back of his head.'

'So he was knocked out?' I asked, chewing a scrap of bacon thoughtfully. Bones pawed at my leg, having been summoned by the smell of food.

'That seems to be the case. I need to ask him again if he remembers anything of what happened, but I fear his state is too fragile.'

'He seems better this morning, though,' chimed Mother from over by the sink. 'A bit more colour in his cheeks. And the doctor said he looked a lot better than he'd expect after a turn like that.'

Well, it wouldn't be difficult for him to look better than he had done last night. He'd been whiter than goose down.

'Does he have any family?' I asked.

Father shook his head. 'I don't think so. I asked him if there was anyone I could contact to say that he was alive, and he said no.'

I felt another pang of sadness for the boy. I stroked Bones gently while his nose crept towards my plate. We would have to cheer him up somehow.

I realised as breakfast progressed that Thomas hadn't woken up yet. When he finally arrived, he walked in yawning and stretching. 'Good morning,' he said cheerily.

I gave Father a quizzical look. 'Does he know?'

'Know what?' demanded Thomas.

'The miracle that happened last night!' I proclaimed.

Mother swatted me with a dishcloth. 'Don't be so dramatic, Violet.' She turned to Thomas. 'There was a small incident in the night . . .'

'A boy who we'd presumed dead,' said Father.

'Who *you'd* presumed dead,' corrected Mother.

'Who *I'd* presumed dead.' Father frowned. 'Wasn't actually dead at all, it seems. Merely deeply unconscious. Your sister found him out of his coffin and wandering the cemetery. A messy business, I assure you.'

Thomas wrinkled his nose, seeming untroubled by the ghastly news. 'How did that happen? Didn't you check first?'

Father gave him his best *stop being insolent or else* glare but it wasn't particularly effective. No matter what facial expressions he made, I always thought he resembled a friendly bat. His round glass spectacles only added to this.

It was a good question. Father was usually so sharp, and did his job perfectly. Was something bothering him?

'We need to get on with the day – there will be no more talk about this at the breakfast table,' said Mother, plonking Thomas's plate down in front of him. 'It's positively unhygienic.'

So we ended the conversation. Mother usually had the final say on these things.

It wasn't until later that I heard my parents talking about Oliver, who had spent another whole day resting. They were in the drawing room, and as I passed the door I heard the mention of his name. I'd be lying if I said I hadn't placed an upturned glass to the wall to hear them better.

'What are we going to do with him?' asked Mother. 'We can't very well just have him live here, can we?'

'I don't see why not,' replied Father, and I heard the *clink* as he put his evening brandy down on the side table. 'I could really use an extra pair of hands. If he truly has nowhere else to go, he might be happy to work for his lodging.'

'We know nothing of his character! He could be a depraved lunatic for all we know.'

I tried not to laugh. And Mother said *I* was dramatic!

'He hasn't done anything to indicate that so far,' Father replied. 'You should think a little higher of your fellow man, darling.'

'But that's just it: he's nearly a young man, Edgar. And he's no relation of ours. What will the neighbours say when they hear of this?'

'They don't need to hear about what happened in the cemetery. Of course Doctor Lane is aware, but we don't yet understand the situation. At the moment the boy doesn't seem to remember anything. Most likely he was just hit by a cart, or banged his head on the kerb.' He paused for a moment. 'What's the harm in telling people that he's a distant cousin?'

'You feel sorry for him, don't you?' Mother asked.

Another pause. 'Well, I feel responsible,' Father said eventually.

'You're so distracted these days,' she chastised him. 'I know things are difficult, but if you wouldn't keep doing funerals for those that can't afford it—'

Father cut her off. 'Who else will, if not me?'

Mother made the tutting, sighing noise that she often made when she knew she was losing an argument. 'Well, dear, I suppose it's up to you. On your head be it!'

Unlike Mother, I wasn't the least bit afraid of what

people thought. What I *was* afraid of, however, was the shadowy face I'd glimpsed at our window. Who could it have been? On the night that Oliver had been found out amongst the graves too. Was that a mere coincidence? The questions buzzed in my mind as I tried to sleep that night. Who had been outside our house? And could they be the very same person who had tried to send Oliver to his grave?

CHAPTER FIVE

Three whole days passed before Oliver seemed to have recovered. At least, he'd recovered on the outside – I was sure he'd never forget the events of that night when we'd found him wandering the graves. I was certain that I wouldn't.

I hadn't had much of a chance to speak with him about what had happened. Any time we found ourselves alone together, Mother would appear and fix me with a steely glare before swiftly escorting him somewhere else.

As soon as he was up and about, Father had broached the subject of Oliver becoming an apprentice – out of his guilt over what had happened, I supposed. Apparently the boy was keen and incredibly grateful (unsurprisingly, since he didn't have anywhere else to go – or if he did, he didn't seem to recall), and Father was already showing him around the funeral parlour. Oliver was dressed in a pair of Father's old overalls, patched brown ones that were tatty and slightly too big but unstained thanks to Mother's overzealous scrubbing.

I watched them both, not saying a word, but silently fuming. I liked Oliver from the brief interactions we'd had, I really did, but I wished Father would pay more attention to my existence. He wanted an extra pair of hands, and I'd always tried to be that for him. I knew more than anyone should about funeral procedures and embalming and coffins. Yet I had the misfortune of having been born a girl, and that apparently meant that I would never be taken seriously. Whenever I told him what I wanted, he would listen to me, stroke my hair, and then tell me that my life was for living, and not to be spent with the dead.

It was all nonsense, really. Why shouldn't a woman be an undertaker? Women brought life into the world, so I didn't see the harm in them helping on the way out. After all, I'd heard that in rural communities it was usually the old ladies who did the duty. They knew the workings of life and death better than anyone.

When I'd told Mother this, though, she had just sniffed and said, 'You may help your father with some matters, of course, but it's really a most improper occupation for a young lady. Who's going to want to marry an undertaker?'

'You did!' I pointed out.

She shook her head. 'You are not your father, Violet,' she said. Then she'd told me to go and finish my embroidery, and that was the end of that.

It was bad enough knowing that Thomas would be allowed to take my place, but a stranger? It was all just so incredibly unfair.

After a while I couldn't stand to watch them any longer. So I went and polished the wooden coffins until I could see my reflection in them and the air was thick with the smell of polish. There were cast-iron coffins too, and some covered in velvet or with elaborate carvings. Some even had what we liked to call 'everlasting flowers' – beautifully made out of lead and sometimes encased in glass. I thought they were lovely.

The weather brightened up a little, so when I'd finished polishing I went to sit outside with my book, on the old bench under the oak tree. Bones lay down beside me, happily chewing a stick. The air still smelled like rain.

I'd just reached the part in the story when Frankenstein tries to re-animate his creation when a hand fell on my shoulder, and I swear I jumped sideways a few feet.

It was Oliver. 'Afternoon, miss,' he said. Bones stared up at him, one ear inside out.

'You may call me Violet,' I replied, trying to sound friendlier than I felt.

He seemed to sense it all the same. 'Have I upset you? I'm sorry if I have. I . . . I don't really know what I'm doing, but I'm proper thankful to your family for taking me in and I thought, maybe . . . um . . . we could be friends?' He sat down on the bench beside me.

I sighed. 'No, no, it's not you at all. It's Father. I wish he'd take me for his apprentice. I know enough!' I glanced around, just in case Mother was about to pop her head out of a bush and chastise me.

Oliver smiled then, a kind, lazy sort of smile. 'I bet he'll see it one day, miss . . . Violet. Something will change.'

'Perhaps if he gets a blow to the head!' I instantly regretted my words, but it spiked some curiosity. 'Speaking of which, if you pardon me asking, have you remembered anything about what happened to you?'

He shut his eyes, as if trying to see the answer in his mind. 'I can remember . . . pain. Here.' He turned and parted the hair at the back of his scalp, where the angry wound was turning to scar tissue. Bones gave a sympathetic whimper from down by our feet. 'Before that . . . I don't know. I know I'm Oliver. My mam died when I was young, an' my pa sent me out to earn a bit of chink by shining shoes. I went to the free school too, run by Miss Blissey, down in Copper Steps? Never did me much good, though. Couldn't get the hang of reading, but I'm decent at sums.' He paused. 'My pa was gone not long after.' He sighed. 'Went off to work one day, never came back.'

I winced at that. 'I'm so sorry.'

He just shrugged. 'At least he might not be dead. But I suppose he thought I could stand on my own two feet just fine.' He leaned down and gave Bones a pat. 'Since then I just did odd jobs for people. I cut lawns with push mowers for grand folk, cleaned windows, an' more shoe shining of course. Then . . . then . . .' He trailed off.

'You don't remember what happened after that?'

'No.' His brows knitted. 'There's a chunk of my life missing. I don't know how long. Could be days, could be years! It's like a fog I can't see through.'

'It'll come back to you, though, won't it?' I asked. I was thinking of how Thomas fell out of a tree when he was five, and couldn't recall how he'd got up there or even what he'd eaten for breakfast. Sometime later it occurred to him that he'd been chasing Ruffian, the big ginger cat from down the street. And it had been boiled eggs for breakfast, he proudly announced.

Oliver lifted his eyelids again and looked at me, and I was pleased to see that his brown eyes had lost their hollow shadows. 'I hope so. I mean, what if I didn't just fall? What really happened?'

'Unfortunately,' I said with a wince, 'we've got no way of knowing now.'

'What do you mean?' Oliver looked puzzled.

'Well, we could have taken a look at the evidence,' I said. 'But, you see, I think someone stole your papers. Your death certificate, the notes on your cause of death and how you were found, everything. At the very least, they're missing.'

'What?' He kicked at a stone in the wet grass. It went flying and Bones tried to chase it. 'Blow me! If that's not suspicious, I don't know what is.'

Now that I'd said it aloud, it did seem very strange. 'You're right there. But Father couldn't have thought it suspicious at the time, or he would have looked into a post-mortem examination.' I watched Bones slink back to us, looking pleased with himself for catching the stone.

'Post . . .?' Oliver began.

'After death,' I explained.

He took a deep breath. I imagined the cool air must

have felt glorious to his lungs. 'I don't really want to think about that,' he said, staring out at the cemetery. 'I . . . I think I need help.' His tone changed suddenly. I could hear the vulnerability in his lowered voice.

'What do you mean?' I asked, picking up the book from where I'd dropped it.

His brow furrowed. 'Well, what if . . . what if maybe someone tried to *kill* me?'

Bones dropped the stone and stared up at him, his head tilted to one side. I was too stunned to say anything.

'I don't know why anyone would want to do that,' he continued, his eyes fixed on the graves in the distance. 'I've never done nothing to nobody. But if they did try to kill me an' they find out that I'm still alive, then maybe they'll want to try again.' He gulped. 'I've been feeling so uneasy, like something *bad* happened to me. An' now this thing with someone stealing the evidence an' all . . . I think I might be right.'

'Murder,' I said, the word hollow in my mouth. 'A real murder attempt.'

He looked up at me. 'That's why I need your help, miss.' I didn't correct him this time. 'I . . . I'm going to need your help to solve my own murder – if I'm going to have any chance of stopping it from happening again . . .'

Chapter Six

My shock at Oliver's unusual request quickly turned to excitement.

'Really?' I asked, clutching my book to my chest. 'You want *me* to *investigate*?' *This could be fun*, I thought. *Dangerous*. Exactly the sort of thing my mother would hate me to do, but that I knew I would love. If they weren't going to let me help out at home, perhaps this was the way I could prove myself.

Besides, it was important. If someone had really targeted Oliver, they could still be out there.

'I've heard you talking to your pa,' he said. 'You're clever, miss, an' you know about all this death stuff.'

I nodded, pleased that he thought that, but I did have my doubts about us going into this alone. 'Shouldn't we go to the police first?'

'Your pa told me not to bother,' he said with a shrug. 'More or less said they wouldn't give two figs about the murder of a street boy who turned out to not even be dead.'

'Hmm,' I replied. 'He does have a point.' Bones poked his head into my lap and I stroked his smooth fur while I considered the matter. 'And of course, if there is a murderer on the loose, it's preferable that they don't know you're still alive. Perhaps it would be better to do this in secret.' The word was more than a little thrilling to me. A secret investigation, just like something out of one of Thomas's Penny Dreadfuls that he borrowed from older boys at school, with their daring detectives and vile villains.

Oliver fidgeted for a few moments, his deep brown eyes staring out at the graveyard. The last of the summer's butterflies landed on a nearby stone, its wings gently opening and closing. 'You're right,' he said finally. 'I shouldn't risk anything. So you'll help me?'

I jumped up. 'Yes!' I said, as Bones barked his approval.

'Of course! You leave it with me. I'll come up with a plan for where to start.'

Now a smile crept over Oliver's face, and his eyes brightened. 'Thank you, miss. You don't know what this means to me.'

'Please,' I insisted once again, 'call me Violet.'

'Very well, miss,' he said with a wink.

I threw the book at him.

* * *

I spent the evening racking my brains for how to start. It was nice to have a real puzzle to keep me occupied for once.

Oliver's words rang in my mind. The missing file: that was indeed suspicious. Perhaps that was the place to start. And the police – even if we couldn't report to them, perhaps they could still tell us something useful.

* * *

The next morning, Bones and I found Oliver cleaning the mortuary, sluicing water over the (unoccupied) slab. He was once again wearing the tatty brown overalls, plus a cap. One of Father's old tweed jackets that he must have had since he was a boy hung on the hook by the door, and I presumed Oliver had been donated that too.

I perched against a rack of shelves while Bones sniffed the floor. He wasn't allowed in the mortuary, but there was no one around to see. Father was out at the stable yard down the street, making sure the horses were seen to. 'I've got a plan,' I said to Oliver.

He looked up at me, then about the room as if a plan were about to appear spontaneously. 'What sort of plan?'

'A plan to find out what happened to you. I think we need to check the filing cabinets. If someone stole your file, then they could have left a clue. And then we need to head for the police station.'

He picked up a cloth and started scrubbing. 'I need to do this first, miss. An' I thought you said we weren't going to the police?'

'Oh, come on!' I grabbed his arm to stop him. 'You asked me to investigate, so you have to trust me on this. We need to get started. If someone wanted you dead, do you think they'll settle for alive?'

He threw the cloth down again. 'All right! All right. I'll help you search through the files.'

I grinned at him. 'Oliver, you're the best dead boy I know.'

'I'm the *only* dead boy you know,' he pointed out.

Once he'd been to take off his overalls and donned the tweed jacket, we went into the shop, and I began pulling open some of the heavy drawers of Father's filing cabinets.

'We need to look where your file was.' I rifled through the O section, peering inside. There had to be a clue somewhere.

'Aha!' I said, pulling out a tiny object that glinted in the weak sunlight.

Oliver stared back at me, bemused.

I quickly realised that I was not holding a vital clue, but a rather deceased bluebottle. Bones hopped up and snapped it from my fingers. 'Ugh,' I moaned. 'Keep looking.'

Oliver leaned over and picked out a random file, waving it up at me. 'What does this say, Miss Violet?'

'It says *O'Connor*. Don't you recognise when it's not your own name?'

He shrugged. 'I didn't go to school for that long. Besides, this writing is all . . .' he made a squiggly gesture in the air with one hand. 'Ain't that a surname anyway?'

I slapped myself on the forehead and shouted, 'Of course! I'm being silly.' Father hadn't known Oliver's surname, nor his first name. 'You were a John Doe!'

He wrinkled his nose. 'Who's that? I don't know any John Doe. They thought I was pretending to be him, or something?'

'No, no, no. That's the name they use for someone who

we haven't been able to formally identify. Father keeps those files at the end of the alphabet.' I rushed over to the cabinet nearest the front window. 'Look, down here.'

I sat down on the wooden floor, in a most unladylike fashion that Mother would not have approved of, and pulled the bottom drawer open. The files that remained had a somewhat ruffled appearance – it must have been from Father rifling through them. But it looked to me as though more than one was missing.

Bones trotted over and began sniffing one of the drawer corners intently, pawing at it. 'What is it, boy?' I asked. As I looked closer, I saw there was a loose nail at the bottom of the drawer, and caught on it was a piece of black lace, a rough triangle shape with a floral pattern. I tugged it out and inspected it.

'Lace?' Oliver asked, wrinkling his nose. 'Is it yours?'

'I don't *think* so,' I said. I couldn't remember tearing any of my clothes. 'Hmm. It could be Mother's, I suppose. She does have some like it.' I stood up again, pulled my purse from my pocket and tucked it inside. 'This could actually be a clue. I'll keep hold of it.'

If the lace didn't belong to me, or to Mother – that meant someone *had* come in and gone through the files in the drawer from which Oliver's had gone missing. It was highly suspicious, to say the least.

‘Good work, Bones.’ I patted the dog on the head, and his tongue lolled out happily.

Oliver still looked puzzled. ‘So we’re going to talk to the police now?’

‘Well, you are,’ I said, though he didn’t seem to notice the implication.

‘Does your ma let you go out alone?’ he shot back.

‘Ha!’ I laughed. ‘What she doesn’t know won’t hurt her.’ I went over to the desk and snatched up a tiny notebook and a pencil. ‘We’ll be back before she knows it. Come on!’

Chapter Seven

Oliver shrugged and then held the door of the shop open for me to pass. I smiled smugly at him and skipped out into the street, holding up my skirts so as not to trail them in the dirt. He looked at me like I was mad, so I gave him a little curtsey and then dashed off in the direction of the shops, Bones rushing alongside me.

Now, this might seem a little eccentric, but you must understand that I very rarely got to escape the confines of the house and Seven Gates Cemetery by myself. Mother thought that the outside world was filled with criminals, and Father would always say that there was a job that needed doing that was more important than going to the theatre, or the zoological gardens, or a tearoom. Whenever I went out, it always had to be with someone else as my chaperone.

So the excursion was a welcome change for me. A breeze was blowing, bringing fresh chill air into the usual city smog, as the chimneys of every house and shop and factory poured smoke into the sky.

Oliver was chasing me, laughing and shouting at me to slow down. I ran with the wind in my hair, speeding around corners and leaping over gutters. Even in my long black dress, I was still fast. Though not as fast as Bones, who had the speed of a greyhound to his advantage and always seemed to know where I was going.

I nearly ran into an elderly gentleman, who stumbled sideways. 'Oops!' I exclaimed. 'My apologies, sir!' I hastily helped him back upright and continued on my way while he muttered curses in my direction.

The police station was not too far away, being within the borough of Seven Gates. I came to a halt in front of it, where Bones stood waiting and panting. The building was a tall and imposing brick affair, with big steps and heavy doors. 'Keep up,' I teased as Oliver finally came round the corner.

'I'm only just back in the land of the living, miss,' he said, gasping as he gripped his knees and panting just like the dog. 'That was a bit much for me.'

'Sorry,' I said. I waited for him to recover before I sprang the news on him. 'So here's the plan. You're going inside.'

'What?' he exclaimed nervously, as a policeman in a tall hat wandered past.

I lowered my voice. 'Say you're a reporter for the local newspaper, and you've heard there might be a murderer on the loose. See what you can get out of them.'

'I don't think I look much like a reporter, though,' he said, pulling off his cap and wringing it between his hands.

I shrugged. 'Well they won't listen to me, will they? They'll say I'm just a girl.' I rolled my eyes. 'Just tell them you're short for your age if they question it.' I pulled out the notebook and pencil and thrust them into his hands. 'Use these.'

'All right,' he said eventually, after a few moments of nervous shuffling, 'whatever you say.' He took a deep breath, and Bones licked his boots for good luck. Then he slouched into the station.

I waited on a patch of grass next to the building. The dew seeped into the bottom of my skirts, and there was a chill in the air, but I paid little attention to it. I threw a stick for Bones to pass the time. When Oliver returned, he descended the steps quickly and handed me the notebook. Bones greeted him with a wagging tail.

I squinted at it. It was a page of unintelligible scribbles. Drat. I'd somehow forgotten that Oliver's reading and writing skills left a lot to be desired.

'Never mind that,' he said. 'That was just to make them think I was taking notes. Got it all up here.' He tapped his forehead.

'Tell me what you found out!'

'Walking first, then talking.' He gently pushed away the dog, who was jumping up to greet him. 'We've got to get back, or your ma will go spare.'

'Come on, Bones, let's go,' I called, following Oliver as he marched on ahead. 'All right, now we're walking,' I said. 'Tell me!'

'The bobby on the desk was a bit distracted, so he didn't really ask questions. I said my name was Jack Danger and that I was a reporter—'

I stopped. 'Really? Jack Danger? Are you serious?'

Oliver smirked. 'Well, like I said, he wasn't bothered. An' I might have slipped him a coin from a couple that your pa lent me. But he said, now that I mentioned it, he *did* recall some similar incidents in recent months. Five people that were not too old, found in an' around Sadler's Croft with blows to the head.' As Oliver spoke, he rubbed his scar subconsciously with one hand.

We hurried along. 'Didn't they investigate?' I asked.

'The bobby said nothing seemed suspicious, especially not for Sadler's Croft. One bloke was at the bottom of some icy steps – they thought he'd had a tumble. One was apparently "riotously drunk" an' holding a broken bottle, so it was a bar fight, they guessed. Two were dragged out of the river. The final one . . .'

He trailed off, and I soon realised why. 'The final one was you? I suppose they don't know you're alive, do they? What did he say about you?'

He shook his head. 'Nothing much. Said I was found outside some toffs' club.'

I stared at him suspiciously.

'I don't remember any of it!' he protested. 'I don't think that's the sort of place I would hang about. I wouldn't steal nothing if that's what you're thinking.'

I had a thought. 'Oliver – all these men were in their prime, with the same sort of head injury . . . could it be that someone was trying to make their deaths look like accidents?'

'But I'm young,' Oliver said. 'So I don't have that in common with those blokes.'

'Hmm,' I said. It was true. Another brick wall.

'That ain't all,' replied Oliver as he went to cross the street, gesturing for me to follow him.

'What else?' I asked. I glanced around, just in case anyone was listening. The way he said it had made it seem rather important.

'All of them – well, excepting me, obviously – are in the graveyard by your house. Your pa did their funerals.'

I wrinkled my nose. 'That must be what Thomas noticed. He said there were several fresh graves. Grown men who weren't old or ill. It does seem strange.'

We turned the corner and were back on my street. The trees that lined it rustled their leaves prettily at us, and the dark branches waved overhead.

There was someone standing outside the shop.

Bones started growling and began to creep forward. With a gasp, I grabbed his collar and pushed Oliver back round the corner.

'What is it?' he said, eyes wide.

'That woman in the black lace,' I said, indicating with a tilt of my head. 'Standing in front of the shop. I've seen her before. I recognise her clothes. On the day when we

. . . found you, she was outside then too, staring. I just thought she was a grieving widow, but—' I shuddered, unable to control it. I could feel the rumbling of Bones's growls against my leg, just as he had growled at her before. He knew something was wrong.

'Black lace?' Oliver said. 'Like we found in the drawer?'

I slowly peered round again. 'It doesn't look quite the same,' I said, remembering the floral pattern, 'and I can't see if there are any pieces missing . . .'

'Maybe she is just a widow then,' he said with a shrug.

'But that's not all,' I insisted. 'Bones growled at her before too. And the night that I found you outside – early on, there was someone looking in through our parlour window.'

He frowned. 'Could that have been her as well?'

I thought about it. 'I don't know. It was hard to see the face, and the figure was only there for a moment. It was night-time, so all I saw were eyes.'

Oliver just stared back at me, and he didn't appear entirely convinced.

I felt foolish. I wasn't even sure now, as I looked across at the woman, that her mourning garb was the same. Ladies in mourning clothes were frequently outside our shop.

However, Bones had a nose for trouble, and he

definitely seemed to think something was wrong. He pulled at his collar, trying to get free. I knew he wanted to give chase.

I peered back to take another look, but the woman was already hurrying away.

Chapter Eight

'We have to follow her,' I said.

'What?' said Oliver. 'No, we don't! We need to get home before anyone notices we ain't there!'

'She must be up to something! Look at Bones!' The dog was straining towards the woman, and I thought my arm was going to be pulled off. 'He knows something's the matter. Come on . . .'

Before Oliver could protest further, I had turned on

my heels and was running after the woman, Bones trotting ahead keenly.

The street was bustling with people going about their daily business, with horses and carts and pedlars, but the woman was tall and I could see the black lace trailing down her back as she darted along the pavement. She scuttled along, and I noticed that she had a jet-black spider brooch pinned to the back of her head, set in a flash of silver. *A Black Widow*, I thought.

I followed in her wake, Bones pulling me until we were near enough to slow down. I hoped Oliver would be close behind.

The woman's face . . . I'd only glimpsed it for a moment, that delicate lace tumbling over her features. But I'd seen a scar, and those eyes . . . they stirred something inside me. I felt as though I'd seen them before, and not just that night at the window.

I saw her pause, and I skidded to a halt, Bones stopping too in a tangle of legs. She was standing beside the cemetery gates, looking up at them. Then she walked through, as if she were going for a leisurely stroll.

I heard panting beside me – and it wasn't just Bones. I turned to see Oliver, his hands on his knees. 'I'm out of shape,' he said breathlessly. 'We're gonna be in big trouble if we don't get back soon.'

I hauled him back up. 'Forget about that. She's gone into our cemetery!' I hissed. 'Let's go.'

Although I had always thought of it as *our* cemetery, it wasn't, not really. It belonged to the City Cemetery Company. It just happened that our house and funeral parlour were conveniently located right beside it, and it had always had a gate that backed on to our land. We had an arrangement, and we spent so much time there that it might as well be ours. I felt strangely protective of it, of anything that might threaten its tranquillity. The woman in black *felt* like an intruder to me, mourning dress or not.

I followed her through the enormous iron gates, beneath the bell tower. Seven Gates Cemetery did not in fact have seven gates (I had counted) – it was just the name of the surrounding area. The graveyard itself was surrounded by a high wall, and those main gates would usually be locked with heavy chains at night, with the only other entrance being through our house. A cemetery was a business, and it was bad for business if bodies went missing. Ours was one of the safest, but grave robbers could be lurking round any corner. What if that was what this woman was doing? Scouting out the place, for her cronies to come in and steal ornaments – or worse?

She wasn't walking quickly, and I didn't want to catch up with her. I merely wanted to observe. I pulled Oliver and Bones into one of the chapel alcoves while she walked up the pathway, which was wide enough for a hearse.

'What are you doing?' Oliver asked.

'Hanging back,' I whispered. 'We don't want her to think we're following her.'

'But we *are* following her,' he protested.

'Precisely,' I shot back, thinking he was being rather dim. He frowned at me, silent and puzzled.

I gazed up into the curve of the archway, where stone angels stared back at me. I didn't come in this way that often, not when we had our own entrance to go through. It was chilly and dark in the shadow of the twin funeral chapels – the more elaborate one for Church of England, the plainer for Dissenters.

Once I could see the woman was far enough along the path, I let Bones off. 'Stay close,' I told him. 'Don't go running after her. Leave this to us.' He tipped his head on one side and then trotted away through the long grass. I knew he wouldn't stray from the cemetery. If I lost him, he'd be back scratching at our gate before long.

I hurried after the woman again, beckoning at Oliver to follow. At one point she stepped off the path and began walking out amongst the stones. I could hear her feet crunching through the newly fallen leaves.

The cemetery wasn't totally empty – there were other

mourners, and even ladies in long dresses out walking arm in arm. Yet the woman in black ignored any she passed, not even offering so much as a 'good day'. She just walked, slowly but purposefully, through the trees. She almost seemed to be going in circles, weaving and twisting, changing direction often.

'She's leading us on a merry dance,' Oliver muttered.

I shook my head. 'I don't think so.' She was heading somewhere, I felt certain of that.

After all, I knew almost every inch of the place, and I knew every resident. I'd say a silent hello to Mr and Mrs Forsyth, to the Abrams family, to the poetic Rossellinis, as I passed their grand tombs, and heard their returning whispers of greeting as a rustle in the leaves. I knew where the broken ash tree lay across the path, where the foxes sheltered in the Egyptian-style Memorial Tunnel, where Josiah Bucket's memorial stretched to the sky. And that meant that I was beginning to realise where the woman was heading.

'Oliver!' I whispered. 'I think she's going to your grave!'

I had to admit, I felt deeply odd saying that. I suppressed a shiver, but the colour drained from Oliver's face. I wasn't sure if it was the memory of the night we found him that was doing it to him, or the thought that this woman could be involved.

It soon became apparent that I was right about her

destination. The woman stopped beside the row of recent graves that Thomas had commented on – where the other men rested. The hole that had been dug for Oliver still hung open, like a gaping maw. Waiting for another occupant, I supposed. It had never happened before. I didn't know what the etiquette was when it came to reusing a space that had been miraculously not needed.

Oliver and I hid behind the trees, watching the woman. I lost sight of Bones, who had slipped into the undergrowth.

She seemed to have frozen on the spot. 'She's surprised,' I whispered. Oliver nodded, eyes wide in silent agreement. I could only see the back of her, but I imagined she was staring down at the hole, wondering what had happened. Anyone would be, seeing an empty grave like that.

As we watched, she took a deep breath, reached into her purse and pulled out five small black roses.

'Black roses,' I muttered, frowning. Those were a bad omen, a symbol of death.

She placed one on each grave, and at the last one, she simply paused, her hand held out over it. Then she snatched it back, and put the rose away again. Her arm was trembling.

Oliver looked at me, his eyes wide. '*She didn't know*,' he mouthed at me.

I raised my eyebrows and nodded back. The woman

in black clearly didn't know that Oliver had come back to the land of the living. But what I could tell was that unless she was some eccentric who paid her respects to the newly dead, the like of which I had somehow never encountered before, the only other thought was that she *did* know all of the victims.

She knew they were dead.

That made her our first suspect for Oliver's attempted murder.

Chapter Nine

We stood and watched the woman for a few moments longer, but we were interrupted by a crunching noise from the undergrowth, and a dark shape coming towards us. I hastily pulled Oliver back behind the tree.

Luckily, or perhaps unluckily, it was just Bones, who began sniffing Oliver's shoes in an enthusiastic greeting. The woman in black must have heard something, and as I peered out I saw her head snap round as she searched for the source of the sound. I held my breath, felt the rough bark of the tree scrape my hands.

Bones turned his attention towards her. I could see the dark hairs standing up on the back of his neck, and he began to give a low growl. I shushed him.

The woman didn't seem to have seen us, but she'd certainly sensed something was up. She gathered her skirts and hurried away.

Within moments she had slipped into the dense trees, and I lost sight of her. By the time we made it to where she had been, there was no way to tell which direction she'd gone in – unless I tried to put Bones on the trail, but I supposed that a large greyhound chasing after her would definitely give the game away.

'Drat,' I said, 'she's on her guard now. And this nuisance didn't help.' I poked Bones gently on the nose, to which he responded by licking my hand.

Oliver shook his head slowly. 'I . . . I thought I didn't want to know what had happened to me. But seeing that . . . that was peculiar. If this was down to her . . .' He reached for his scar. 'Or she knows who did this to me . . .' His words trailed off.

I put a gentle hand on his arm. It *was* strange. We would just have to investigate further. But how?

I turned to Oliver. 'Let's head for home. I would say Father will be dreadfully worried that we've been gone for so long, but his head is in the clouds these days . . .'

* * *

The following day dawned, and I woke with the ferns of the first October frost creeping up my window.

Mother insisted I help her peel potatoes for a pie, grumbling about how much she missed the cook. Bones hovered about our feet, hoping for scraps. Father and Oliver were out working that morning, yet I had been forbidden from joining in, much to my annoyance.

I had other things on my mind. Namely, the woman in black with the spider brooch in her hair. We needed a plan, yet we knew nothing about her, save for the fact that she hung around the cemetery like a bad smell. What she was doing there, only the dead knew.

As I thought that, I paused, my knife halfway across a potato. If the dead knew . . . perhaps they would tell me?

And so, once I got the chance to slip away from house duties in the middle of the afternoon, I made for the back gate and headed out among the gravestones. Bones happily picked up a stick and bounded along beside me.

In the past I had never had much luck with talking to ghosts. Feelings and snippets of words were all I could usually manage. But this was a new matter. A dangerous investigation – *murder most foul*, as Thomas had put it. Would they now have more to say?

I first made my way through the sparkling dew of the melting frost back to the row of graves, each topped with a single black rose and with the empty hole at one end. I glanced around, but there was no sign of anyone – mysterious woman in black or otherwise.

'Spirits,' I called, unsure how else to address them. I reached out my hands towards the mounds of earth. 'Um . . . were you . . . murdered?'

Nothing happened. I could hear birdsong and the wind in the trees, and felt nothing but cold.

'Did you see the woman in black?' I asked the empty air. 'She left you flowers? Do you know what she's up to?' I closed my eyes and listened. I thought I heard the wind pick up, felt tiny pinpricks of cold go down my arms, but that was all.

I heard a bark and turned to see Bones harassing a pigeon. 'Here, boy,' I called. He bounced back over to me and curled around my legs, panting. 'Make yourself useful. Can you hear anything?'

The dog tipped his head, an ear pricking up, and whined.

I huffed and sat down beside him in the wet grass. I had to try harder.

I put my gloved hands down, and just tried to concentrate, to *feel* with every ounce of my might.

There was *something* there . . .

I felt a sudden warmth in my fingertips. The world seemed tinted red, and I heard the crackling of a fire and the hint of words on the edge of hearing.

Avenge us.

Justice.

I shuddered, and opened my eyes, and suddenly I was back in the chilly October graveyard with Bones sitting in front of me. He blinked his dark eyes slowly.

Try as I might, I could feel nothing else. The ghosts had said their piece. Whatever it meant, I knew one thing – they were angry, and someone had made them that way.

Chapter Ten

I followed the path back down the hill, stopping along the way to touch gravestones and ask about the mysterious woman – but the dead were quiet that day. I caught echoes of curiosity, and yet none seemed desperate to tell me anything.

Halfway down I stopped for a rest, leaning against Mrs Jennings's gravestone. She had been dead fifty years, and she didn't seem to mind. I felt a faint warmth against my back as I sat – not the angry warmth of the fiery spirits, but almost like a ray of sunshine on that cold October day. She was welcoming me.

I peered out round the stone, and I caught sight of Oliver coming up the path. Bones jumped up and ran over to him.

'What are you doing, Miss Violet?' he asked, dodging the greyhound's affections.

'Investigating,' I replied, not wanting to explain that I was attempting to converse with ghosts. I wasn't sure that it would be well received.

'Really? Have you found anything?' Oliver sat down beside me in the grass, before thinking better of it. 'It's all wet!' he exclaimed, jumping back up again. 'How are you not soaking?'

'I'm wearing three layers of petticoats,' I said, climbing up and pulling Bones's lead from my pocket so I could attach it to his collar. 'And no, unfortunately.'

'No more sign of that woman in black?'

I shook my head. 'I think we scared her away.' I waited as a few more ladies wearing mourning clothes ambled past up the path, arm in arm. 'Perhaps we need to call her something more specific. Like . . .' I thought of the spider brooch perched in the back of her hair, and the way she crept around. 'The Black Widow.'

Oliver shuddered. 'We'd better get back,' he said. He

rubbed his stomach, probably thinking of the potato pie. 'Your family are wondering where you've got to.'

I paused for a moment. *My family*. That was a thought. Over the years, I had found that my connections with family ghosts could be stronger. 'Hmm,' I said. 'That gives me an idea. Come on.' I began striding ahead towards the other path that led down through the row of mausoleums.

I came to the last one and stopped, placed my hand on the carved upside-down torch on the doorway, and whispered a few words. It was a regular ritual. 'Here we are,' I said.

When I turned, Oliver was watching me, hands wedged in his pockets.

'What's this?' he asked.

I looked back at him, wondering why it wasn't obvious, before I remembered he couldn't read.

I waved up at the inscription above the door. 'It says VEIL,' I said.

Oliver peered at me. 'You think it has something to do with the woman in the veil?'

'No, you clod! It's our surname!' Honestly. Did anyone else do any thinking around here? 'It's our family mausoleum.'

He raised his eyebrows. 'Your family are . . . buried in here?'

'Not *buried*. Oh, never mind, I'll just show you.' I

reached into my dress and pulled out the brass key from where it hung on a chain round my neck. I unlocked the door, gripped the heavy iron ring and pushed it open. There was barely a creak. I tied Bones to the ring. 'Wait here, boy,' I said. 'We're going in.'

For a moment, Oliver stood frozen. I wondered if it was too uncomfortable for him, given what had happened. 'It's dark,' he said.

I thought perhaps he just needed a little encouragement. I gave him a gentle shove and he stumbled in. 'Oi!' he said playfully. 'Watch it!'

I grinned at him. 'Welcome. I know it's dark. They don't really have any use for windows.'

I gestured around at the walls as Oliver stared up at them. The mausoleum was about the size of a large garden shed, with thick shelves going all the way up. On the shelves rested several stone coffins of varying sizes.

'This is Grandfather,' I said, pointing at the one on the top right.

Oliver seemed to think something was expected of him. 'Pleased to meet you, sir,' he said.

'And this is Grandmother,' I said, pointing to the other side.

'Ma'am,' Oliver said with a cheeky smile. He tipped his cap at the coffin.

‘She says good afternoon,’ I relayed to him as an echo of a warm voice rattled in my ear. I wondered if he would be concerned by the idea that I could hear whispers from the dead, but he seemed to take it in his stride. I wondered if perhaps he thought I was joking.

‘Why ain’t they next to each other?’ he asked.

I laughed at the thought. ‘Grandmother said he was a cantankerous old hoot when he was alive, and that she’d be blowed if she had to spend eternity right next to him as well. Apparently he snored too.’

I felt what could only be described as a grey wave of grumpiness, and fought back the urge to laugh again. Grandfather never changed – he was stubborn even in death.

Oliver grinned. ‘That’s where you inherited the bad temper from then, miss?’

‘To borrow one of your terms,’ I said, ‘*oi*!’ I turned and ran my finger along the shelf, expecting dust, but there was none. This place was as sealed to dirt as it was to time. There was nothing but a tiny spider scuttling into a crack in the stone.

‘I’m going to try something,’ I said carefully. ‘Asking them a question.’

Now he looked at me with curiosity. ‘All right . . . Don’t think you’ll get much answer, though.’

I turned, put out my hands to the walls and closed my eyes. 'Have you seen a woman in black? Acting strangely in the cemetery . . .'

A faint blue tinge spread across the darkness beneath my eyelids. The colour of mystery. I felt the rough stone under my fingertips crackle.

Strange.

Familiar. I spoke the words out loud as they came, but my voice didn't sound like my own. *Someone close.*

'What does that mean?' I asked. Were they saying I knew her? That she was nearby?

Cold... witch, my grandfather's ancient voice said suddenly in the back of my mind. It made me shudder, but I wondered if he was talking about the woman or insulting my grandmother.

Before I could ask more, the sounds of a far-off argument met my ears, and the voices slowly drifted away.

'Ugh,' I said, opening my eyes and clenching my fists in frustration.

Oliver was staring back at me, open-mouthed. 'You can . . . hear the dead?' he asked finally.

Now, the thing was that this was something I had held on to for so long because nobody had ever believed me when I told them, so I had given up mentioning it. I went quiet for a moment, wondering if he was about to tell me that I had an overactive imagination, as my parents always did when I so much as hinted at what I could see and hear.

'Yes,' I said.

'So . . . what's it like?' he said finally, his words a soft breath of fresh air.

'A feeling,' I replied with relief. 'Emotions. Sometimes muttered words or sentences. I wondered if I could hear anything at the victims' graves back there, but all I felt was a desire for . . . revenge. Justice.'

'How do you do it?' Oliver asked, his eyebrows narrowed, questioning.

The question caught me off-guard. No one had ever asked me that before. I thought about it. 'I don't know.' My gaze ran over the coffins. 'I think people leave echoes when they go. You can't drop a stone in a river without making ripples. I think perhaps I can feel the ripples.'

I often thought that about Bones too. Dogs had better senses than people, didn't they? Perhaps the ripples were even clearer to him.

Oliver shivered again, properly this time. The chill was pouring in from outside, and he hadn't the warm clothes that I had.

'Ain't you ever . . . sad? That people are gone?' he asked.

I smiled at him gently. 'Of course I'm sad. But it's part

of the cycle. Look!' I grabbed his sleeve and pulled him back out of the door, into the bright orange light of the sunset. He shielded his eyes. 'Look around you.' I waved my hands. 'When I first understood death, when I started to cry about it, Father brought me out here. It was autumn, just like it is now. He said to me: *The sun is setting. The leaves are falling, the flowers are bowing their heads. Do you cry for them?* And I shook my head and sucked my thumb, and he asked, *Why not?*'

I turned and pulled the door of the mausoleum shut, locking it behind me, tucking the key away safely again in my dress.

'I thought about it, and I said . . . *Because there will be new ones*. And he told me I was right. A new sun would rise in the morning, new leaves would grow on the trees, new flowers would bloom.'

'The spring comes,' Oliver said quietly.

I smiled again, brushed the wet ground with my feet. 'No matter how long and how dark and how cold the winter, the spring always comes. The autumn has to happen to make way for the new life. That's what he told me. He said the autumn happens, and we're here to sweep up the leaves.'

There were a few moments where we said nothing, just stared out over the cemetery, as the dying light bathed everything in orange and pink. 'He's clever, your dad,' Oliver said finally.

'He is,' I said. I breathed out, a cloud of mist in the frosty air. 'Come on. We should get back. There's pie.'

CHAPTER ELEVEN

The following day was when I first heard whispers of murder.

Father's footsteps were already moving about the house when I woke. He called out to Mother and asked where he'd left his hat – he had a funeral that morning.

Oliver was coughing outside. He was lurking about in the hallway beside my door as he waited for Father – I could see the shadow of his ill-fitting shoes in the crack beneath as he shuffled in the morning light.

I was planning on seeing if I could get involved in the

arrangements – not least for a chance to get out of the house and perhaps do some investigating. Mother helped me into my corset and dress, but I knew she was expecting me to stay inside and to either do housework or sit around being ladylike, and she would kill me if she found out what I was really planning to get up to. *Oh well*, I thought. *At least I'll get a decent funeral.*

Once Mother had gone down to the kitchen I waited quietly and listened for Father and Oliver's hurried foot-steps on the stairs – I knew they would be heading out to make sure that the coaches and horses were all in order. Together with Bones, who was slinking down the stairs beside me, I was going to see if I could sneakily follow them. I pinned a hat to my hair and fetched my coat from the stand.

But as I exited the front door of the shop, I heard something that I couldn't possibly ignore.

'*Murder!*' a well-dressed lady gasped from a few feet away.

Bones's ears pricked up, and if I'd had a greyhound's ears, I suspect mine would have too. Time seemed to slow for a moment.

'Oh yes,' said a different lady from behind her fan. 'Shocking, isn't it?'

I bounded over to them. 'Wait! Who's been murdered?'

But my efforts were fruitless. Both ladies looked at me with disdain and hurried away up the street towards the entrance of the cemetery.

'Ugh,' I huffed, glancing down at Bones. He inclined his head towards them and whined. 'You're right,' I said. 'We need to investigate. This could be connected to what happened to Oliver and the others.'

With a quick bark, Bones bounded off. With absolutely none of the caution that I knew I should have had, I hurried after him.

Today's event was for an older man, however, not a young man – a taxidermist named Mr Walcott who had lived on Rathbone Street. Father had told me that last night. I soon realised that Father had underestimated Mr Walcott's popularity. The street outside the chapel was filling up. The crowds parted a little to let us through – being accompanied by a large black greyhound often had that effect.

Black-clad mourners lined the pavement – mostly men, but there were groups of women too, like the ladies I'd heard speaking of murder. I had to get more information – find out if this was a potential victim of our culprit. I sidled up to a suited man who was standing alone, smoking a pipe. He had frown lines that suggested a near-permanent scowl.

I pulled out a freshly starched black handkerchief and sniffed loudly. 'Ooooh,' I wailed, blowing my nose as I patted Bones dramatically. Sure enough, the man scowled at me, looking rather disgusted. I had his attention, at least. 'It's just so dreadfully sad!' I sobbed.

'Here for old Walcott, eh?' the man said gruffly, looking away from me. I often noted how uncomfortable men became when ladies were being hysterical.

'Gone too soon,' I said, waving my handkerchief for effect. 'What a . . . what a *man* he was! And such a wonderful . . . taxidermist!' I broke into racking sobs as the suited man tried to edge away from me.

He exhaled a cloud of angry smoke into the autumn air, his frown still heavily plastered on. 'He wasn't much of a man. He was a gambler and a cheat, for my money. Knew him, did you, lassie? I don't think most of this lot did.'

I dabbed at my eyes. 'I was . . . merely a fan of his work,' I said. 'Are we not surrounded by his doting friends and family, mourning his tragic . . .' I paused, unsure if I should try it, and then barrelled ahead anyway: 'murder?'

'Ha!' The man nearly dropped his pipe, and Bones jumped. 'Not likely. He choked on his fish and chips, or so I heard. This lot are just here because of the rumours.'

He laughed, not a happy laugh, and then walked away, shaking his head.

I frowned at the pavement, thinking. *The rumours?* What rumours? If Mr Walcott was no victim, then was he a murderer himself? Could Mr Walcott have been the villain we were looking for?

But as I was lost in these thoughts, Bones brought me back to earth with a thud as he began desperately pawing at my leg.

I looked up – and it was then that I saw her.

The Black Widow.

It was only for a moment. A flash of her eyes beneath black lace as her head turned, the spider clinging to the back of her hair in its lace web. She was walking through the crowd on the other side of the street, holding something – pieces of notepaper, it looked like.

I stood, as if in a daze, watching as she handed one to a nearby lady who had just arrived. The pale lady read it, looked briefly horrified, and then folded it into her purse. They exchanged a few whispered words before the Black Widow tucked her papers away inside a tattered deep red notebook.

I was still debating whether to follow her when I noticed that Bones had made the decision for me.

'Bones!' I hissed. 'Come back!' But it was too late. He

was trotting through the crowds towards her as she turned and began to head for the chapel. I had no choice, did I? I had to follow them.

I stepped off the pavement, and a horse reared up beside me, its carriage driver pulling to a halt.

'Oi!' the driver cried in a gruff voice. 'Watch where you're going!'

I paid him no mind. I was on the case!

I reached the pale lady and tugged on her sleeve. 'What did she tell you?' I demanded hurriedly.

She just shook her head, eyes wide. 'A murderer in our midst!' she said, without looking at me.

I wanted to ask more, but Bones was still following the Black Widow. I could just see him up ahead, trotting paws in hot pursuit as the gossiping mourners parted to let her through.

She's going into the funeral, I realised.

I left the pale lady where she stood, and ran after the Black Widow.

Or at least, I tried to run. It was like swimming through treacle – people got in the way of every step. When I finally reached the entrance to Seven Gates cemetery with its grand chapels, the Black Widow had vanished.

'Did she go inside, boy?' I asked Bones, who had stopped.

But Bones was sniffing and poking at something on the ground. A crumpled ball of white against the dirty brown of the pavement.

'Good boy,' I said as I reached down and picked it up. Had the Black Widow dropped it? It was a couple of torn pieces of paper, so I picked the ball gently apart and flattened it against my dress. I could tell it was a page from a journal, perhaps the one that the Black Widow had been holding.

The first read simply, in angry capitals:

IS A MURDERER

It was ripped off at the top, so I didn't know who it was accusing. Was this what she had shown the shocked lady in the street?

But the second piece was neatly ruled and handwritten in a way that suggested either keen precision or madness. I read the words.

I put my trust in you. I thought you would understand. You knew a love like the light of the sun, as I did. I did what I had to, to survive – for more than survival. For a life.

But then you took the sunshine from me. And all was dark. We froze in the winter. Everything I loved was taken. Now you too will know the feel of the cold.

★ ★ ★

My skin prickled all over. This could mean nothing good.

I hastily crumpled up the journal page and hid it away in my dress. I would have to show this to Oliver.

A sound rang out over the streets then, a low, mournful clanging. The chapel bell was tolling. I looked up.

There she was, all in black, slipping inside the chapel.

'Oh no,' I said to Bones, and to the world in general. 'We're going to have to follow her, aren't we?'

CHAPTER TWELVE

I needed a disguise. Thinking quickly, I unfolded the black handkerchief and tucked it into the brim of my hat, making a makeshift veil. It wasn't very convincing, but it at least hid my eyes from view.

I was about to run inside when the crowd swarmed around me, with the swishing of many ladies' skirts. The funeral procession had arrived, and was lurching up the street beside us. Everyone was huddled together, a cloud of gossip and whispers. *Nosy lot*, I thought as I pushed in between them. Then I lifted my veil to get a better look.

There was the large black mourning carriage. I recognised the coachman driving the horses as Mr Dreyfuss, who had the most fantastic bushy moustache, like a broom that had taken root beneath his nose. He wore his silk hat at an angle, the long black crape weeper cloth descending over his cloak. He was tipping the hat at people in a jaunty fashion as he passed, which I felt fairly certain he wasn't meant to do.

The horses were black, too, of course. Father liked to tell people that their names were Orpheus and Eurydice, which I suppose he thought was more fitting than their actual names, which were Daisy and Buttercup.

Managing to grab hold of Bones's collar, I watched as the procession slowed even further to make the turn through the chapel archway and through into the courtyard. I caught a brief glimpse of Father and Oliver riding a carriage, and tried to hide behind an exceptionally wide man in the hopes that they wouldn't spot me. When I looked out again, I could see everyone descending from the carriages and hopping out on to the cobbles. The pallbearers went to the back of the hearse to start shifting the coffin.

Everyone began moving towards the chapel, and I tried to listen to what they were saying, but the chatter had grown louder as soon as the procession passed, and it was hard to filter the noise.

'Did you see him?' I heard someone say.

'I wonder if it's true?'

'Someone really ought to tell the police . . .'

What has the Black Widow been telling them? I thought. *Did she accuse old Mr Walcott? And why? If we could only catch up with her, perhaps I'd be able to find out.*

I decided to try on Oliver's accent, dropping more of my Hs and Ts. ''Ere,' I said to a nearby woman, who moments before had been whispering to her friends. 'You 'eard these rumours, then?'

The woman's eyes lit up. 'Oh yes,' she replied. 'Me and Bessie here, we love a good scandal!' Bessie giggled. 'We just couldn't believe it when we heard! We had to come down and look. With all respect to old Mr Walcott, of course, God rest his soul.'

Hmm. This was going to be more difficult than I'd thought. How was I to extract information about the rumours?

I twisted the hem of my lace through my fingers. 'Was 'e a good man?'

'Oh no, he was a gambler and a cheat, the old goat,' said the woman. 'But that's nothing, is it! Not to murder!'

'Ha!' Bessie laughed again, and I wondered why she was laughing. But before I could say any more, the two women bustled away.

I was swept along with the crowd as it poured towards the twin chapel, the Church of England side. I pulled the lace back down over my eyes and tried my hardest to look as though I definitely belonged there, although it seemed most of the crowd weren't friends and family of the deceased any more than I was. Or if they were, they didn't seem to be particularly sad about his passing. There were plenty not even dressed in mourning black – cooks in floured aprons and tailors in patterned waistcoats with their scissors. They all seemed to be there to watch the spectacle.

As I neared the entrance, I noticed the men began to split off.

Ah, yes, I thought. Although I'd never been allowed to go to a funeral before, I'd been inside the chapels many times, sneaking in at night to get a good look around. There was a gallery at the back for the ladies, with a screen across to protect our delicate feminine eyes or something of the sort.

One of Father's men was at the door, greeting everyone. *Blast.* It was Mr Patel, who had known me since I was knee high. Thank goodness for the veil. But I had to say something, or I wouldn't get in. And what about Bones? I was still gripping his collar tightly, the back of his tail swishing against my legs.

I loosened my grip for only a second but as soon as I did he shot away, slipping amidst the sea of black-clad funeral-goers. 'Bones!' I hissed, but it was too late. He bounded through, getting caught on a long black scarf as he went, its lady owner gasping as it wrapped round him. Then he disappeared from view, vanishing into the chapel. *Oh no!* I thought.

Well now I had no choice. I *had* to go in.

After a quick whispered prayer to whoever would listen, I moved forward with the crowd.

'Welcome,' said Mr Patel, giving me a small bow.

'Uh . . .' I said, racking my brains, ' . . . *bonjour? Je suis* . . . *très* . . . sad,' I mumbled, dabbing at my eyes.

He tilted his head sympathetically, and waved me inside.

I couldn't believe that had worked.

I stared up at the vast Gothic ceiling of the chapel as we entered, but I quickly remembered why I was there. *The Black Widow.* Would she be heading to the gallery, or lurking in the shadows? There was a surprising amount of noise – I was certain people were meant to be quiet and respectful at a funeral, but instead everyone was chattering. They were doing so in lowered voices, but the effect was like a cloud of murmurs hanging over the room.

The coffin wasn't in yet, but some of Mr Walcott's taxidermy creations had been placed at the front by the altar, including a tea party of rabbits and a rather unimpressed-looking black cat.

I hung back by a pillar and looked around, desperately searching . . . There she was. Over the other side of the chapel, near the stairs to the women's balcony, in her long black dress and lace. There was a glint as the spider brooch at the back caught the light.

Just as I was about to move towards her, I heard a familiar voice from the door near the altar.

'Bones?' It was Oliver. He must have been sent in to wait until everything was in place, at which point the undertaker's men would usually go outside.

I stood on tiptoes and saw Bones was right at the front of the chapel, scarf hanging over his face, enthusiastically greeting Oliver. I saw a few people pointing at them. *Oh no.*

Where was Father? That was something I didn't know about funerals – where the undertaker would be while it was all going on. I could only see Oliver, who looked baffled as he petted Bones, turning his head as if trying to see where the dog had appeared from. He pulled at the scarf and tried to throw it over the dog to hide him, but Bones wiggled free.

I leaned round the pillar and waved at Bones, hissing his name. His ears pricked up, and I tipped my head towards the Black Widow. 'Over there!'

Perhaps I was overestimating the intelligence of my dog, but I felt certain that he would know to come back to me so that we could track the woman. Unfortunately, he had other ideas.

Time seemed to stand still as Bones leaped into action. He bounded past the stuffed cat, sending it flying into the lap of a bespectacled man in the front row, and clattered up the aisle. The woman in black spun round with a gasp, only to find herself knocked to the floor by an overzealous greyhound.

Now that the lady's veil was askew, I could see that she had a sea of freckles and not a scar in sight.

She also looked extremely surprised.

I realised, with increasing horror, that it was not the Black Widow.

'Sorry!' I called out, as the entire congregation turned and stared at me. 'Bad dog!' I winced and hurried over to pull Bones off her.

It was then that I felt a sturdy hand on my shoulder.

'You, young lady, are in *big trouble*,' a voice hissed in my ear.

Well, that answered my question.

Father was right behind me.

And he looked *furious*.

CHAPTER THIRTEEN

Father marched us outside to the courtyard where the funeral carriages were now standing. Bones whimpered, his tail between his legs. He knew he'd done something wrong. *'This is all your fault,'* I hissed down at him.

Oliver had slipped out of the side door and was now waiting in the shadows. He tipped his hat at me politely.

'Oh, don't give her that,' Father snapped. 'Not after the mess she's just caused!' He turned back. 'Are you going to explain yourself? A funeral is NOT the place for a girl.'

Well, there went any notion I had of telling the truth. If Father thought I was too delicate to even look at a funeral, what would he say if I told him I was on the trail of a murderer?

'Perhaps I just wanted to see a funeral for once,' I said, wrenching my arm free from Father's hand. 'You let me help out at home all the time, but I'm never allowed to come here. It doesn't make *sense*.'

When Father was truly angry his face would turn pale and drawn; his eyebrows knitted so tightly, his brow furrowed. That was precisely the face he was wearing that moment.

'And why in heaven's name did you bring the dog?'

I bit my tongue. 'Um. He followed me?' Bones whined in agreement.

Father looked completely unimpressed. 'Your antics might have just ruined my reputation, do you understand? How dare you behave in this manner!'

'S-sorry,' I tried, as Bones cowered behind me. 'I don't think anyone recognised me, my face was covered, I . . .'

Unfortunately, Father showed no interest in my apologies or explanations.

'Oliver,' he growled. 'Take her home.' He turned to me. 'I'll deal with you later.'

Oliver took my arm, but his grip was so light that it

barely registered. I thought he seemed uncertain whether he was more afraid of my father or of me.

'But Father—'

'But nothing, Violet. This is my profession. There is no excuse for letting your wayward behaviour put everything I've worked for at risk! Now, go! Mr Walcott isn't going to bury himself!'

Before I could say anything more in my defence, Father was storming back into the chapel.

A cold breeze blew up, swirling the autumn leaves around us. Oliver dropped my arm. 'Sorry, miss,' he said. 'What were you really up to?'

'I was following a lead!' I grumbled back, feeling a little perturbed that he had seen through me that easily. I waved towards the chapel. 'I saw the Black Widow go in. I was trying to chase after her. But then Bones had to go and jump up at the wrong lady.'

Bones simply stared upwards, and I got the sense that he was cross with me too.

'All right,' I huffed, 'I thought she was the Black Widow as well, but it was just some poor lady with a spider brooch. They must be in fashion. But the real Black Widow was there, trust me. I saw her outside. Everyone was talking about murder. I thought they must have been referring to old Mr Walcott, but then I saw her. And she dropped this.'

I handed him the crumpled notes as the colour drained from his face.

'I can't . . .' he started, and I realised I was being foolish again.

I read the writing on the piece of paper out to him but it didn't do anything to improve his complexion. 'What does it mean?' he asked quietly. 'This is really odd. And who is she accusing?'

'I don't know,' I said. 'I don't have the part that was torn off, and I didn't hear any names. That's why I was hoping to catch up with her.'

He stared back at me for a moment, as if weighing up whether to ask a question, but he eventually asked it. 'Why didn't you tell your pa the truth about why you were there? That you were investigating?'

I kicked at the dust with my shoe, making Bones jump and scuttle behind Oliver. 'Because he wouldn't understand, would he? You heard what he said. *A funeral is NOT the place for a girl.*' I made a face. 'He'd have a fit if he knew what I was really up to.'

'Well, funerals ain't much fun, miss,' he said, petting Bones.

'I know that,' I snapped back. 'But they let you do it. Nobody looked at you and said "he's just a boy, he doesn't belong there, he's too delicate . . ." Did they?'

'No.' Oliver's mouth twitched half a smile. 'Maybe they should have.'

'Ha! Come on.' With a tilt of my head I gestured for us to start walking. If Father re-emerged, he wouldn't take kindly to me hanging around like a lost urchin. 'Here's the thing. People look at you, or Thomas, or Father, and they see a person. They look at me and all they see is a *girl*.'

We emerged through the gates between the chapels, and out into the street. It was less busy now, with many having gone inside, but there were people standing around – still gossiping, by the looks of it. Bones trotted along at our heels, seeming slightly miffed.

Oliver nodded thoughtfully, considering my words. 'When my pa sent me out to shine shoes, I remember we passed a shop lad, from one of the big places. He was all dressed up in a fancy uniform. I asked my pa – "why can't I work in a shop, like him?" an' he just shook his head, said "That ain't for the likes of us, son. You'll shine shoes or you'll starve." Maybe he was right. But he . . . he put me in a box.'

'What do you mean?' I asked as we made our way down the street, Bones trotting alongside us.

'He put me in a box I didn't want to be in,' Oliver explained. I fought the urge to mention his brief time in a literal box. 'Or maybe the world put me in it. It seems to me you're in a box too.'

'That's just it,' I said. 'If I solve this case, and find out who tried to murder you . . .' I waved the mysterious notes, 'it won't just make sure you're safe. It might just mean I can break out of my box.'

'But how are we going to do it?' He frowned, staring down at his feet on the cobbles. 'Get to the bottom of all this?'

I gripped the papers tightly in my hand. It worried me too. We needed to find more to go on. 'I don't know,' I said, 'but we must.'

When we arrived back at the shop, Mother was in quite a state.

'Violet!' she shrieked as we came in the front door. 'Wherever have you *been*? I've been so worried. I've had Thomas scouring the cemetery for you!'

The truth was teetering on my tongue, but I knew Mother wouldn't understand any more than Father had. 'I tried to go to the funeral,' I said with a shrug.

Mother put her hands on her hips and just stared at me, speechless. 'Young lady,' she said. 'I don't know that I'm surprised, but I'm certainly not happy. What were you thinking?'

I turned to Oliver, but he was staring at his shoes. Bones was sniffing the floor. No help at all.

'I'm just naturally curious, Mother,' I tried. 'I thought you said a little curiosity was healthy in a girl?'

'*Yes*, Violet, but your curiosity is positively morbid!' She slammed her hand down on the desk, making a sheaf of papers jump. It was quite unlike her to do so. 'You've disobeyed us, and gone gallivanting around on your own. Do you know what could have happened to you?'

I could have died, I thought. *Then perhaps they'd let me go to a funeral.* But since I valued my life, I didn't say that aloud. 'I'm sorry, I truly am.'

'Sorry isn't good enough this time,' my mother said. Her face was set in stone, and I knew she meant it. 'You will go to your room until your father comes home.'

With a huff, I strode towards the back of the shop and out into the corridor. Bones trailed along behind me, his tail between his legs.

A few seconds later, I heard Oliver's voice pipe up from behind me: 'Excuse me, ma'am, but am I in trouble too?'

I stopped, one foot on the stair.

'No, Oliver,' my mother said in a defeated voice. 'You're not in trouble. Go and sweep up, will you?'

'In the suit, ma'am?'

'No, I . . . just go away, Oliver.'

'Yes, ma'am. Sorry, ma'am.'

As Oliver trudged away to the funeral parlour, I stared

down at the notes in my hand. This could be a lead, and I knew I was going to have to follow it.

I may have been in big trouble now, but little was I to know at that moment that just round the corner, more trouble was waiting. If I was going to prove myself to the world, I would have to face it, head-on.

CHAPTER FOURTEEN

The trouble was going to catch up with me sooner rather than later. Upstairs in my room, I heard Father clatter through the main door to the house. I quickly hid the mysterious torn paper under my pillow and picked up my embroidery.

He pushed open the door. His arms were folded, and he stared at me wordlessly. That was never a good sign.

I put the needlework down very gently, as if Father were gunpowder and the slightest spark might set him off.

'I'm sorry,' I said quietly, but I couldn't hide the waver in my voice.

'Violet, listen to me now.' He walked into the room. 'You must stop this foolish behaviour. You cannot interfere with my work. Do you understand?'

'Yes,' I said quietly.

He started to pad up and down the floor, the way that Bones would do. My nightstand wobbled beneath his heavy footsteps. 'You may not have a governess to discipline you any more, but you must discipline yourself – learn to *have* some discipline. It isn't only your reputation at stake. It is our family's, and the business's. And we can't afford to lose those.'

I picked the loose thread even harder, and bit my lip. 'Do you care more for the business than for me?' I asked quietly. I was pushing my luck, and I knew it.

'Oh, Violet. You mustn't talk that way.' He sighed and sat down next to me, stroking a lock of hair back behind my ear. 'You know how important you are to us. But the business is important too. It's how we afford to eat. To own our home.' He paused, and I wondered if he was about to tell me something, but he seemed to blink his thoughts away before continuing. 'Without it, we could easily be the poor fellows in the morgue. You have to understand that.'

Now it was my turn to sigh. 'I understand.'

'Good.' He got to his feet again, brushing off his hands on his coat-tails.

'But . . .'

He turned to look at me, and his expression asked, *What now?*

'I still think it isn't *fair.*' I stood up beside him. 'I should be allowed to do more.'

'And you will be allowed to do more, when it is appropriate. But you'll soon find that often life isn't fair. Was it fair to everyone out there?' He waved his hand in the direction of the cemetery. 'Do you think so?'

I shook my head slowly. I knew most of them. There were plenty of waves of sadness and emptiness that I felt out among the graves, of love and loss.

'Life happens. We live the way we must. I'm telling you, this is the way *you* must live. It keeps you *safe.*'

This time I nodded. I had more arguments, more ways to disagree, building up on my tongue – but I couldn't let them spill out. This was the end of the conversation. I wouldn't get another chance. 'I'm sorry, Father.'

He gave me a gentle nod in response, and then went to leave, before appearing to think better of it. He came back over and put his hand on my shoulder. 'You stay in your room and think about it,' he said. 'You'll do wonderful things, my girl. I know you will. Violet Victoria Veil. A strong name, like the queen.' He smiled, and it looked odd against his funeral get-up. I felt my heart grow a little warmer.

I just hoped that he wouldn't find out what I was really up to.

The next day, I spent the first few hours of the morning confined to my room, unsure when I would be allowed to come out. Mother helped me to dress in angry silence, and had Thomas bring me breakfast. I then sat alone, with Bones sulking on the end of my bed.

I do despise being confined, but I wanted to use the time wisely. Since no one was keeping an eye on me, I pulled out the mysterious notes and pored over them.

'We're stuck, boy,' I said to Bones. 'How are we going to find out what that woman is up to? How is it all connected?'

I went over to my dressing table, took out my ink pen and diary, and began jotting some notes.

The Black Widow – did she steal Oliver's file?

Does the black lace belong to her?

Why did she go to the old man's funeral?

Did she drop the notes?

Why does she write of love and someone taking something from her? Is she spreading the rumours accusing someone? Who?

I felt as though all I had were questions, with the answers far out of sight. But what could I do?

Bones whined at my feet, padded over to the door and began scratching at it. 'You're right,' I said. 'We need a plan.'

INVESTIGATION PLAN

Track down the Black Widow – dangerous

Ask the ghosts for help – difficult

Discover identities of the other victims – impossible!

Nothing to go on!

I threw my pen down in frustration, sending splatters of ink across the table. How was I to do any of this if I couldn't leave the house?

My grumpy solitude came to an abrupt end, though,

when a bubble of commotion floated up from downstairs. Bones's scratching became more frantic.

'*All right*, boy!' I said. I had to go and see what was going on. If anyone objected, I'd just have to tell them that Bones needed to be let out.

I flung open the door, picked up my skirts and ran down the stairs. Bones hurtled ahead, his footsteps clattering as his paws hit the wood. To my surprise, Father was pacing the hallway at the bottom, running his hand anxiously through his hair. I could hear banging and shuffling from the funeral parlour. Bones stood beside it, growling and shaking.

'Father?' I asked. 'What's going on?'

'Violet?' He turned, his face white with surprise. 'Get back upstairs, my dear . . .'

'I know I'm supposed to stay in my room,' I began, 'but Bones—'

'No,' Father said, leaning down and putting his hands on my shoulders. 'I don't mean because of the punishment. The police are here. They're searching the place.'

'Why?' I asked, my brows knitting.

Father stood straight again, taking off his spectacles and rubbing his eyes. 'They said they had a warrant to investigate. Murdered men who all came through here . . .'

I gasped. 'You mean Oliver's case?'

'Yes,' he said, glancing around furtively while the

banging continued in the background. I heard the gruff voices of policemen in discussion. 'I just sent him out to the stables. But yes, I think it could well be.'

'But I don't understand,' I said, wringing the fabric of my dress through my hands. 'We just did their funerals; what evidence could they find here—'

'Please, just go back upstairs, Violet,' Father said firmly, but at that moment, the doors that led to the funeral parlour opened, and two police constables came striding out. Both had sombre moustaches, and even more sombre faces. One of them was holding something heavy, wrapped in paper. The other held a pair of handcuffs.

Bones backed towards me, still growling. I took his collar in my hands. Something was wrong.

'Mister Edgar Veil?' one of them said.

Father turned to them. His hands were shaking.

The constable held up the object, and as the paper fell open, I caught a glimpse of dirty metal. *A hammer.* 'We have reason to believe that this was the weapon used in the Seven Gates Case.'

'What?' I whispered. 'No . . .'

Within seconds, the other constable had grabbed Father's hands and pushed them behind his back, the spectacles clattering to the floor. 'We're arresting you,' he said, 'on suspicion of murder.'

Chapter Fifteen

I couldn't believe the words I'd just heard.

Suspicion of murder.

'W-what is the meaning of this?' I demanded.

The first policeman looked down his nose at me as if I were a gnat buzzing around his face. 'And who are you?'

'Miss Violet Veil. I'm his daughter.' I looked frantically at Father, whose face was still pale, eyebrows drawn.

'You ought to keep quiet,' said the second. He roughly grabbed Father's hands and clicked the handcuffs round his wrists, locking them tight. 'This is a serious business. I suggest you keep those lips shut.'

Just then, another man strode through the doors from the funeral parlour. He was tall and imposing, wearing a tweed overcoat and a waistcoat with a watch chain neatly dangling from the pocket.

The first policeman tipped his helmet at the man. 'Inspector.'

I stood unmoving as the man sized up my father with his gaze. Bones kept growling, that low rumble that spread through his chest, as he tried to pull away from me.

'Mister Veil,' the man said. His voice was quiet but commanding. 'I am Detective Inspector Holbrook. We have reason to believe that you are responsible for the murder of five people.'

I gasped, and a sense of dread crept over me. All that talk at the funeral earlier, the gossip, the whispers, the staring eyes . . . The word *murder* had been in the air. But it wasn't old Mr Walcott they were talking about. It was Father!

That was who they had been waiting for in the streets.

'No,' I said, but it came out as a feeble whisper. 'Father . . . he wouldn't do anything like that.'

Father just stared at the hammer. He looked as though he were about to be sick. 'I've never . . . that's not mine,' he said weakly.

They were wrong about another thing too. There

wasn't a fifth victim. Oliver was alive! *Surely* he would have known if Father had been the one to attack him? He could tell them Father was innocent.

But he wasn't there. Father had sent him out.

'Oliver! Mother!' I called desperately towards the back of the house, hoping that someone, *anyone* would come along. I pointed Bones in their direction. 'Fetch someone, boy,' I begged, and he pulled free and bounded out.

My outburst caught the attention of the inspector, and he walked slowly towards me. 'Young miss, is this your father?'

'Y-yes,' I stuttered, cursing myself for stumbling over my words. 'He wouldn't do this!'

'That's what they all say,' I heard one of the constables mutter.

'I didn't,' Father said, his voice low and weak. 'I've done nothing wrong. I swear. I didn't even know they were murder victims,' he added with shame. 'Accidents, the coroner said.'

The inspector ignored him. 'Young miss,' he said again. He had a formal tone, but there was something in his voice that I found worrying. It reminded me of a snake waiting to strike. 'This is a grave matter. We believe your father has committed terrible crimes, and we need to take him in for questioning. Is your mother here somewhere?'

I shook my head, unable to find the words. I didn't know where she was.

The inspector slipped me a printed card. 'Well, when you find her, you tell her to come and see us.'

'What . . . are you . . . basing this on?' I asked. The words clawed their way from my throat. 'You can't possibly . . .'

'We have enough to arrest him,' the inspector said plainly. 'We received an accusation.' He gestured at the hammer, which the other constable was wrapping up again. 'And now we have the murder weapon, which matches the crimes.'

Shocked and ashamed, I started to cry. 'Please don't take him away,' I said, gasping. It felt as though the air was being stolen from my lungs.

There was an ounce of pity in the man's expression. 'We do what we have to,' he said. Then he clicked his fingers and marched out towards the shop.

I followed, but I was powerless to help as the constables led Father outside. His eyes met mine, and they seemed to be silently pleading. Through the shop window, I watched them drag him along the street until they were out of sight.

'I'll help you,' I said tearfully to the empty window. But there was no one there to hear.

* * *

When I'd finally found my feet, I wiped the tears from my eyes, picked up Father's fallen spectacles, and ran through to the house. 'Mother! Oliver! Thomas!' I called up the stairs. 'Anyone?' There was no answer. Where were they? Bones came clattering back to me, looking as confused and hurt as I felt.

I found the back door shut – Bones hadn't been able to get out to look for them – so I flung it open and ran out into the yard.

Mother was there, hanging washing on the line. She looked calm and quiet, a wooden peg in her mouth and two in her hands. For the tiniest second, I didn't want to break her blissful ignorance, but there was no other way.

'Mother!' I cried.

She took the peg out. 'Don't shout, Violet, I'm right here,' she said. 'Anyone would think—'

'Father's been arrested!' I interrupted. Bones barked mournfully.

Her expression froze for a moment. 'Violet, if this is some kind of jape . . .'

'It's not, I swear it!' I panted, putting my hands on my knees. 'Two policemen arrived, and an inspector.' I waved the card at her. 'They said he was accused of murder, and they found a hammer, and they took him away!'

Mother threw the washing into the basket and stepped towards me. 'Slow down, Violet; what did they say?'

'Someone's accused him, Mother. Of murdering the men in the graveyard. They think he murdered Oliver too, because they don't know he's alive!' I straightened up. 'And they found a hammer that they said is the murder weapon, but it can't be Father's, he said he'd never seen it before. We have to do something. We must go down to the station, right away!'

Mother had gone unusually pale. 'Are you certain?'

Of course I'm certain, I wanted to say. *It happened in front of my very eyes.* But I was too afraid for that. Instead, I simply nodded. 'We . . . we have to help him, Mama.'

I hadn't called her Mama since I was about five years old. Suddenly I felt like a small child again. Helpless. Afraid.

'Where are Thomas and Oliver?' she asked.

'I don't know! Not in the house,' I said. 'Perhaps they're at the stable yard.'

Mother quickly abandoned the washing. 'Come on,' she said. 'We'll find them and go down to the station. I'll get this cleared up straight away. It *must* simply be a misunderstanding.'

I clung to her words – in that moment, they were my only hope.

* * *

We found Thomas and Oliver at the stable yard as I'd thought, tending the horses. Mother, with the calm manner of all mothers who are suffering something terrible, bent down to talk to Thomas.

'I need to go out somewhere with your sister. Stay in the house,' she ordered. 'Don't let anyone in.'

'But—' he started, with a jealous glance in my direction.

Mother put a finger to his lips. 'It's very important. Stay here, keep an eye on Bones. Can you do this for me?'

Thomas looked like he was about to protest, but after taking in the expression on Mother's face he apparently thought better of it. 'Yes, Mother,' he said, before wiping his hands on his trousers and heading for home.

'What's going on, miss?' Oliver asked.

For some reason I couldn't put the whole explanation into words. It was Oliver's worried eyes and wringing hands. He knew something was wrong. 'We need to go to the police station, right now,' was all I managed. 'I'll explain on the way.'

Chapter Sixteen

We hurried through the streets, me clutching Father's spectacles in my hand. Mother had stopped talking. I could tell all the worries in the world were going through her head. Murder was a very serious charge. It meant the death penalty.

I was trying desperately not to think about it.

Father's a good man, I told myself. *It's all just a misunderstanding. We'll have him out by the end of the day.*

The constables hadn't listened to me, but then I was *just a girl*. With Mother and Oliver to back me up, they would surely change their minds. I'd eventually found the strength to explain to Oliver what had happened, and he was now marching along with us in silent resolve.

When we reached the station, Oliver suddenly stopped at the bottom of the steps.

'What is it?' I asked him. I watched as Mother bustled up to the doors ahead of us.

'They'll probably remember I said I was a reporter called *Jack Danger*,' he hissed.

'Drat,' I said. 'You're right. I was hoping you could tell them you weren't a victim, and that Father didn't hurt you.'

He winced and rubbed his head. 'I'm sure he didn't, miss, but . . . I don't remember nothing.' His frown crushed a little of my hope. 'I'm not certain it'll help, not if there's four other blokes dead and buried.'

I squeezed my hands into fists and let out a cry of frustration. 'Come on,' I said, grabbing his arm in a most unladylike fashion. 'We have to go in anyway. If they think you're a reporter, it might help.'

I pulled him up the steps until we were both through the doors.

The foyer was fairly large, with a solid desk across the middle. A man in uniform sat behind it. It was quiet, with only a couple of policemen standing around, and a few queuing people who looked in varying levels of mild distress. Mother gave them a quick glance before obviously deciding that our distress was greater. She approached the desk.

I went up beside her while Oliver tried to hide behind me. Mother's hand was shaking. I took hold of it.

'Excuse me, sir,' she started.

For a moment, the policeman didn't even look up. 'One moment, madam,' he said, slowly entering something in flowing handwriting in a log book.

'It really is quite urgent,' she said. 'My husband—'

'One moment, please,' he repeated, barely meeting her eye. He carried on writing, and her hand tremored all the more. 'You'll have to wait your turn.'

I glared at him. He had beady eyes and a flat nose. How dare he make us wait?

Then I had an idea. I stepped back and shoved Oliver forward.

Instantly, the man looked up, his expression brightening in recognition. 'Oh, Mr Danger, is it? Back for another story?'

Mother's face was a picture. I was fairly certain mine was too.

'Err, the same one, actually,' Oliver told him. He seemed to straighten up then, as if putting on the role like an overcoat. 'The one with the murders. I heard there was a development.'

'Oh yes,' said the policeman. 'Well . . .' He cleared his throat. 'I can tell you that we have arrested a man in connection with those murders. If you need my details, it's Sergeant Andrew Wilberforce. With one L.'

'Right, yes, of course, thank you . . .' Oliver said. The sergeant didn't seem to notice that Oliver wasn't carrying a notebook or pen, nor the fact that there was straw on his jacket and that he smelled slightly of horse. 'But these ladies here—'

'We met him outside,' I interjected.

'Yes, um, they're the wife and daughter of the man you've arrested. So can you tell us more about who has accused him?'

'Oh,' said the policeman, with the merest glance at us. He seemed to find our presence about as interesting as a long-dead rat in the gutter. He leaned forward over the desk and spoke in a quieter voice to Oliver. 'We received an anonymous tip-off.'

'You would see my father hanged on *an anonymous tip-off*?' I exclaimed, but Mother shushed me.

'It was fairly detailed, and it placed the blame on the accused for the deaths of the five victims,' the policeman continued. I wanted to protest again, to tell him that there weren't five deaths – the fifth person was right beside us. But that would blow Oliver's cover, and it was the only thing getting the man to talk at that moment. 'Said he killed them with a blow from a hammer, and covered it up. We searched the accused's property, and found the hammer in question. Probably no chance of bail for this one. That's all I can say for now.' His beady eyes twinkled. 'But you will put my name in the article, won't you?'

The man spoke as if his words weren't just like a hammer blow to all of us. I felt sick. Either Father had been arrested for murders he didn't commit, or he'd been framed. There was no possible way that he could be the monster who had done this.

'You don't honestly think,' I said, stepping up to the desk, 'that Edgar D. Veil, undertaker, a man with the most intimate knowledge of death and the deceased, would be so careless and obvious as to murder people with a *hammer*? He would do better than that!'

'Violet!' my mother snapped, appalled.

The sergeant blinked at me. 'I would watch what you say, little miss,' he said darkly.

'It just cannot be true,' I insisted. 'The hammer must have been planted. Father said it didn't even belong to him. Maybe he found it and was just using it to fix up a coffin – he needs all manner of tools. It doesn't mean a thing!' I slammed my fist down on the desk, making everyone jump.

'Please excuse her, sir, she doesn't know what she's saying.' Mother's glare shot through me like a bullet. 'She's distressed. We all are. Please, will you let me see my husband?'

The sergeant gave a weary sigh. 'All *right*, madam. He's down in the cells. Follow me. Will you be joining us, Mr Danger?'

For a moment Oliver said nothing, and then suddenly realised he was being spoken to. 'Oh, yes,' he said. 'Of course.'

I took a deep breath, steadied myself.

I had to stay calm. Father needed me.

We followed Sergeant Wilberforce down a set of gaslit stairs, so narrow that we had to walk one at a time. It almost felt as though we were descending into another world. Brick arches rose over our heads, the light flickering across them.

At the bottom, the passageway widened a little, and I could see a corridor stretching away before us, with that same high arched ceiling. The ghostly lights illuminated a set of sturdy-looking black cell doors, each with an opening hatch cut into the wood. I gave Oliver a worried glance, and saw my anxiety reflected in his own eyes.

'Here,' said the sergeant, stopping outside one of the doors. 'You get five minutes. I'll wait here. No funny business, all right?'

We shared a sideways glance, and remained silent.

He unlocked the door and slid back a heavy bolt. As I peered inside the cell, I couldn't help but gasp.

It was a tiny room, with whitewashed brick walls. There were few furnishings besides a cracked latrine and sink in one corner, a simple desk and a hammock. And there on the grey flagstone floor, with his head on his knees, was Father.

It was as if I heard a tearing in the world, felt it beneath my feet, but I blinked my eyes and there was nothing.

Father tilted his head towards us, slowly and bleary-eyed, but soon scrambled up when he realised who we were.

'Go on,' the sergeant said, pushing us into the tiny space.

Mother hesitated for a moment, before rushing forward and throwing her arms round Father's neck. Oliver and I stepped inside with trepidation. There was only room for us to stay just inside the door. I heard a clank as the sergeant swung it shut behind us. I felt as though we'd just been sealed inside a tomb.

'Oh, Edgar,' Mother sobbed.

I felt the cell walls pushing in on me and sank back against the cold stone. I couldn't think of a single reason why Father would commit murder, no matter what the police thought. I gently handed Father's spectacles back to him when Mother let go. He took them and put them on. I couldn't find the words.

'The charges aren't good,' Father finally said.

'*Aren't good?*' Mother exclaimed. 'Edgar, you could be hanged!'

Father's face was the colour of sour milk. 'I know, Iris,' he said again, a hint of desperation in his voice. 'But I didn't do this, I swear. I didn't do what they said I did.'

'Of course not,' she said, wiping her tears with her handkerchief. 'Of course not.'

Oliver stepped forward. 'Sir,' he said. 'We'll find a way to help you. I don't know who hurt me, but . . . I'm as certain as Violet that it wasn't you. You're a kind man, and I just . . . I don't get any bad feeling from you, even if I can't remember what happened. I mean it, we'll get you out of here, sir.'

'Thank you,' said Father flatly. His eyes looked empty. I knew he was worried and that he didn't believe that Oliver had anything that could help. I wasn't certain if I did either.

Oliver turned to me in desperation. 'The Black Widow . . .' he muttered.

I flinched at the mention of her. In all the commotion, I'd almost forgotten. 'We need to find her,' I said.

Mother turned to look at us. 'Who?'

'Nothing,' I said quickly. I didn't want to explain, nor was I sure if we really knew anything beyond our suspicions and the fact that she'd been lurking in the shadows. Perhaps we were clutching at straws, but they were the only straws we had right now.

Mother's eyebrows narrowed, although she stayed clinging to Father. 'What are you up to, Violet? And why on earth does the policeman think that Oliver is a reporter?'

Summoning my courage, I took a small step further into the miserable cell. 'We still don't know what happened to him.' I waved towards my friend. 'That's not to mention the poor souls lying in the cemetery. That's why I went to the funeral yesterday. I was investigating, because I thought it could be connected to them all. There were people spreading rumours of murder.' I shuddered, thinking of the context those words now had. 'The police have got it wrong,' I added. 'I feel sure that if we can find out the truth of how Oliver came to us, we'll find the key to who's behind this.'

Oliver took a deep breath. 'I pretended to be a

reporter to get some information, ma'am. I'm helping her investigate.' He winced a little at Mother's expression. 'Sorry, ma'am.' He turned to my father. 'Sir, is there anything you can remember about the victims that might help us?'

Father let go of Mother. He rubbed his temples in frustration. 'I should have noticed . . .' he muttered to himself. 'Well, they all had head wounds. The coroner . . . he dismissed them quickly, thought they were the usual Sadler's Croft drunkards. He said the cause of death was obvious. They'd all fallen and hit their heads . . .' He frowned as he said it, as if he was only now unsure of what he'd been told.

'But they were all, in fact, murdered,' I said. 'Which means the murderer is still at large. And whoever they are, they've falsely accused you.'

Father's frown deepened.

'Can you think of anyone who'd want to do that, sir?' Oliver asked, taking well to his interviewer role.

'No,' Father said quickly.

'Please,' I begged him, stepping closer. 'Is there anyone who might feel wronged or—'

'I said NO, Violet!' he snapped.

I felt my whole body tense. 'But . . . Father—'

'I must forbid you from investigating,' he said. 'This is

not one of your games. This is not a trivial matter. This is my life . . .'

I felt my eyes prick with tears. 'That's why I'm trying to help!'

'I will not discuss this.' He flung his hand out, making Mother jump this time. 'You will not go running after murderers. It's foolish and dangerous. Do you understand?'

Now my mouth just flapped open uselessly. This was the only way we might be able to help Father. What else could we do?

'I said, do you understand?' Father demanded.

A shuddering breath filled my lungs. 'Yes.'

'Edgar,' my mother said gently, taking his hand.

I felt the first tear fall down my cheek.

We were interrupted by the sergeant entering the room. 'Time's up,' he said.

I wanted to protest, but the fight had gone out of me. I closed my eyes, wishing more than anything that I could see Father smiling and wishing me goodnight, and not standing there empty-eyed against the cold walls of a prison cell.

When I opened them, I watched Mother slowly pulling away from Father . . . could almost feel her pain as she dropped his hand. Father slumped back against the cell wall, like a clockwork marionette winding down for the last time. He said nothing as we left.

The sergeant turned and deadlocked the door, with a final *thud*.

I couldn't help feeling, as we made our solemn procession back up the stairs, that I might have lost my father forever.

Chapter Seventeen

Mother cried silently all the way home. I couldn't think of a single comforting word to say to her.

I didn't cry any more. I couldn't. I had to stay strong, and if I started, I knew I wouldn't be able to stop. Yet as we walked, I became convinced of something. Something that was slowly burning its way through my veins.

I felt sure I could get to the bottom of this and free my father. Whatever it took.

Of course, he had just expressly forbidden me from

doing any sort of investigating. And yes, he would be furious if he found out. But he was trapped in a prison cell, and if I did nothing he might never see the light of day again. Or worse, he would face the hangman. If I could do something, *anything*, then I was going to. Once he was safely back with us, he could be as furious as he wanted.

My mistake had been to try and talk to him about it. I prayed I hadn't ruined my last moments with my father. How could I have been so foolish? I ought to have kept my mouth shut. Around Mother too.

At least I had Oliver. Together, we could prove Father's innocence. That was what I kept telling myself, so that I could put one foot in front of the other.

It began to rain, spitting cold down on us. It seemed appropriate.

We eventually arrived back at the shop. We'd left in such a hurry that we'd forgotten to lock up.

'Wh-who's there?' came a small voice from behind the desk.

Mother wiped her eyes and peered blearily. 'Thomas? Didn't I tell you to stay in the house?'

As I approached, I saw that my little brother was sitting in Father's chair. He wore a pair of Father's spectacles, and was holding Bones's collar tightly with one hand while grasping one of our miniature coffin samplers in the other. Bones whimpered quietly.

'Nobody was in here,' Thomas said, a little shakily. 'I thought there might be customers. I was . . . I was being responsible.'

'Did anyone come in?' I asked, my voice low.

'Um, yes,' he said, letting go of Bones, who circled the desk to greet us, wobbling with either nerves or excitement. 'A lady. But she went away again.'

Mother just put her hand over her forehead and sighed, but I was immediately concerned.

'A lady? What did she look like?' I asked.

Thomas frowned. 'I don't know. She had lace over her eyes.'

Oh no. 'Did she say anything?'

He shook his head. 'No. But the dog didn't like her. He was growling.'

Horrified, I grabbed Oliver's arm.

'That doesn't mean much,' he whispered as Mother gently chastised my brother for not doing as he was told. 'Almost every lady who comes in here wears a veil.'

'And doesn't speak?' I hissed back. 'Bones growled, he must have recognised her!'

Oliver shook his head, unconvinced. But *I knew*

it was her. What could her motivation be? Was she stealing something? Covering her tracks? I almost felt as though she were taunting us. I shuddered at the thought that she had come in with Thomas here alone.

'Where have you been?' Thomas asked. 'Where's Father?'

I winced. Bones was staring at the door, sniffing and sweeping his tail as if he was waiting for Father to walk through it at any moment. I knew that he wouldn't, that perhaps he never would again.

Mother breathed in, deeply, for too long. She went over and put her hands on Thomas's shoulders, and then she finally spoke. 'Your father has just had to go away for a little while, Thomas. But don't worry, my dear, he'll be back soon.'

'Where's he gone?' Thomas asked. His eyes were wide, and I could see tears in them.

Mother looked over at me, and I felt another horrible wave of helplessness. I didn't know what to say, either.

She cleared her throat. 'He's had to go down to the police station,' she said quietly. 'It's to do with work. He'll be back soon.' She glanced at me again, a wordless plea not to tell him the truth.

Thomas jumped up, sending the chair clattering backwards. 'You're lying!' he shouted.

'Thomas . . .' Mother started, looking too desperate to even be angry.

Thomas wasn't listening. He ran out towards the back of the house, Bones galloping in pursuit. He knew when someone needed comforting – and of course he liked a good chase.

Mother stood up again slowly, and I could see she was shaking.

'Leave him,' I said, going over to her. 'He'll be all right. You need to sit down.' She didn't resist as I helped her into the chair.

'Ma'am,' Oliver said. 'I know this ain't the time, but . . . what about the business?'

'I can help run everything,' I said. 'I know everything that needs to be done. I—'

'Violet,' Mother said wearily. 'You know the answer. Young girls are not undertakers.'

'But—' I protested.

She reached for a glass of water on the desk and took a sip, the glass shuddering in her hand. 'Not today,' she said. 'Do not argue with me today, Violet.'

'She has a point, miss,' Oliver said.

I turned to him, my hands on my hips and a frown of silent indignation. Oliver thought I wasn't up to the job as well?

He read my expression quickly and fumbled for a better answer. 'You've got the book knowledge well enough, but there's more to it than that. It's hard work. Sad work.' He broke off, swallowed, then tried again. 'I don't know how your pa does it all. I don't think I can do it. Not yet. Not alone.'

Mother bit her lip, and I could see the tears threatening to spill from her eyes.

For a moment, I said nothing. I couldn't meet Oliver's gaze.

'You're right,' I said eventually. 'We can't do it without him. We'll have to close.'

Oliver fiddled with the buttons on his jacket nervously. 'The men can probably do the rest of the funerals for this week. But after that . . .'

I slammed my hand down on the desk, making both of them jump. 'There won't *be* an "after that"! We're not leaving him in there! I'm going to get him out, whatever it takes.'

'Violet, remember what your father told you,' Mother cautioned.

'I'm not likely to ever forget it,' I shot back.

She raised a finger at me, but we were interrupted by the front door of the shop opening.

'Hello, everyone!' came the cheery voice, and the wet *thwoomp* of an umbrella being shaken out.

I spun round. 'Maddy!' I cried with relief.

It was our maidservant, back from her trip to Yorkshire. I ran over and threw my arms round her.

'Oof! Goodness,' she said, a warm smile on her freckled face. 'I think you've grown again, Miss Violet.'

I let go of her, and her eyes widened as she saw Oliver. 'Hello,' she said again. 'Who's this?' Then she must have noticed Mother sitting solemnly at the desk, because she asked: 'Is something wrong? What's going on? Where's Mr Veil?'

The stream of questions made Mother start sobbing again.

'Maddy,' I said, gripping the sleeve of her coat. 'Something's happened while you were gone.' I caught Oliver's eye, and took a deep breath. 'Well, a lot, in fact. You might want to sit down . . .'

By the time I'd recounted the whole story, Maddy was sniffling and wiping her eyes with her handkerchief. 'I just can't believe it,' she kept saying. 'Not Mr Veil. How will we manage without him?'

Maddy was eighteen and pretty in a way that she never noticed and men always did. She had a friendly, open face framed with wild curls that she tried in vain to tame. It was awful to see her friendly face on the verge of tears like this.

'I'm sorry, Maddy,' I said. 'You've only just come home. And there's nothing we can do.'

She sniffed and stood up. 'Don't you go apologising, Miss Violet. It'll do no good.'

'You can call me Violet,' I said, as I always did, but Maddy paid it about as much attention as did Oliver.

'You're quite a miracle, aren't you, boy?' she said to him. He just blushed and looked away.

'Right.' Maddy straightened her skirts and turned to my mother. 'There must be a lot to be done. Just let me know, ma'am, and I'll get started.'

Mother took a deep breath, and then she climbed to her feet too. 'Come along to the kitchen,' she said.

As Mother drifted away, Maddy looked back at me and placed a hand on my shoulder. 'You know in your heart that he's done no wrong, don't you, miss?'

'Of course,' I said.

'Then there *is* something you can do,' she said quietly. 'Come and speak to me tomorrow once I've helped your mother. I'll tell you what I know.'

CHAPTER EIGHTEEN

The next morning was a sombre one. Even Bones seemed out of sorts. I let him out of the back gate, only to have him solemnly stare back at me from the graves instead of going for his usual bounding run.

The front door of the shop had remained locked, the desk unoccupied. Mother had hung a sign on the door that read –

CLOSED DUE TO UNFORESEEN CIRCUMSTANCES. PLEASE RETURN AT A LATER DATE.

It wasn't going to be good for business, that was for sure: the dead don't wait around for an undertaker. Everything must be sorted as quickly as possible. That meant that all our potential customers would be heading straight for our rivals, Flourish and Co.

But however bad for business it was to be closed, I felt sure that the rumours would be worse. I'd peered out of the front window to see a gaggle of girls around my age pointing at the shop, whispering and looking horrified. I couldn't hear their words, but the gossip from the funeral filled the space well enough. I knew what they thought of my father.

I turned to find Oliver sitting in the back garden in the weak sunlight, whittling a piece of wood with a small knife. 'Good morning,' I said, not even convincing myself. 'Haven't you got anything to do?'

Oliver scrambled to his feet. 'Not at the moment, miss. There's a funeral for tomorrow, and several for the rest of the week, but then all the . . .' he cleared his throat . . . 'coffins we have will be . . . used.'

'The people buried, you mean?' I said.

He winced a bit, and sat back down again. 'Yes. Sorry. The work is good and honest but . . .' He took a deep breath, as if he wasn't sure whether to continue. 'But I can't stop thinking that it could have been me, miss. It chills me to the bone.'

Bones came trotting back in, probably thinking his name had been mentioned. He sat at Oliver's feet and put his head in his lap.

I patted Oliver gently on the shoulder, once I was certain that Mother wasn't there to see. 'That's another reason why we need to get to the bottom of this. We need a plan, Oliver.'

I was expecting him to argue, so I was a little surprised when he nodded in agreement as he absent-mindedly tickled Bones behind the ears. 'You're right. What are you thinking of?'

I rubbed my hands together for warmth. 'Maddy said we could talk to her. Father may not tell us anything, but I think she will. She's worked here for a few years – she knows him well.'

Oliver agreed. 'We've got nothing to lose there. So long as your ma don't find out, course.'

'Hmmph!' I snorted. 'It's not exactly dangerous investigating, is it? It's just talking to Maddy. I don't see how she can tell me off for that.'

We found Maddy in the corridor upstairs, frantically dusting. She looked hot and flustered. 'I don't know where all this came from!' she was muttering. 'I wasn't gone for long!'

I sidled up to her, Bones squeezing along beside me. 'Maddy, you said we could talk to you?'

She brushed a lock of hair from her face and glanced quickly down the corridor, then she tilted her head towards the stairs to the attic. 'Come on then – five minutes. Up there.'

We hurried after her as she dashed to her bedroom (Bones was always happiest when people were moving quickly). Oliver hesitated on the threshold, but I dragged him inside.

Maddy's bedroom was plain but homely. She had a quilt that had been sewn by her mother spread across her bed, and some needlepoint pictures that I'd made for her hanging on the walls. There was a rather wilted flower in a jug by her bed, probably from one of her many admirers. Bones tried to jump up on to the bed and she quickly shooed him off and sat down herself.

Oliver took out his notebook and pencil, but I tapped them meaningfully with a finger.

'Remind me to teach you to write,' I said. 'Or those won't be any use.' I turned back to Maddy as his cheeks reddened. 'What did you want to tell us? Can you help me prove Father innocent?'

She folded her arms and bit her lip. 'All right . . .' she began. 'I know you'll have been told not to get into this, but I also know *you*, Miss Violet, and that you'll stop at nothing. So if there's anything you can do with the things I've heard . . .' She sighed. 'Perhaps it'll help you.'

‘Please,’ I said urgently, ‘if you know something about who might be responsible for this . . . Anyone who might have a grudge against him for any reason?’

‘I might,’ she said, still looking uncertain that she should even be telling us about this. ‘Do you remember Mrs Brean?’

‘Oh, of course!’ I said. Mrs Brean had been our cook for years, before Father had to let some of the servants go. I’d really liked her. She was tall and skinny, which seemed unusual for a cook, but she always had a jolly outlook on life. Plus her cooking was wonderful. Mother – bless her – was not so used to the task.

Maddy pulled on a lock of her hair, her eyes seemingly focused on the past as she tried to recall it. Bones stared up at her, unblinking.

‘When I first came to work here, she told me about something that had happened with one of the other staff.’ She paused, fidgeting uncomfortably. ‘Maybe she was gossiping, or it was a warning to me – I wasn’t sure. But she said things started to go missing. That someone was stealing.’

‘She didn’t say who it was?’ Oliver asked, leaning forward eagerly with his notebook. Maddy shook her head.

‘Go on,’ I said. ‘What sort of things went missing?’

‘Leftovers and food at first, but then some household

things. A few valuables and clothes, even. Mrs Brean said it was right strange. Nobody ever saw anything being taken. But then Mr Veil must have found out who it was, because a woman was sacked.' She winced. 'The others had to be let go, difficult times and all that, and of course that was awful, but it was all on good terms. Whoever *she* was, Mrs Brean thought she got sacked for certain. Very messy apparently.' She got up. 'I'll say no more. I must get back to the dusting.'

Sacked? I thought. Being sacked was much worse than being let go. It meant that the servant couldn't get another job. I didn't remember anyone being sacked – but then perhaps it was at the same time as the others were let go. In which case it could be any of them.

I didn't remember hearing about any thefts, either. Had it been kept from us? 'Does Mother know about this?' I asked, before Maddy could run back to her dusting.

Maddy shrugged. 'I don't know. I don't think so. Mrs Brean said it was very hush-hush. I think she overheard Mr Veil dismissing the lady.'

Oliver looked at me. 'Well, if your pa was the one who sacked her . . . it would give her the perfect motive to falsely accuse him,' he said.

Chapter Nineteen

The very idea that one of our former servants might have falsely accused Father was so disturbing, I found it hard to think about.

Our servants had always felt like a part of our household, of our family, even those who may have sometimes been cold or harsh when I'd got under their feet a few too many times. These were people we had shared our home with. If it was true, that one of them had been stealing from us and was now targeting Father . . . how could they betray us in this way?

I racked my brains as I tried to think back through all the women who had worked for us – which wasn't so many compared to the older, richer families further along the street like the Winstons and the Braithwaites. There were the maidservants, the governesses, the cook . . .

I remembered our Nanny Mishka, who looked after us until Thomas was about five. She always wore brightly coloured plaster jewels over her black dresses and told us fascinating stories about animals and mystical markets where you could buy anything from singing butterflies to potions that made your hair curl. I was sure I could rule her out – she had a sweet and pleasant nature, and the last I'd heard she'd boarded a ship to the Americas. And if our sacked servant was indeed the same person as the Black Widow, Nanny Mishka looked nothing like her.

Mrs Keaton, the housekeeper, was just as keenly engraved on my memory. She was always a sunny presence, which wasn't easy in a family so deeply surrounded by death. The business never bothered her – she acted as if all we did was sell pretty flowers for a living. I was devastated when she left, and would have been surprised to hear if she'd harmed a fly.

As for the others . . . I was losing track of their names.

Some of them I thought must be too young. Maddy had said a woman, not a girl.

I felt sure, though, that we had records of who had worked for us. They would be amongst Father's files in his office at the back of the shop, surely?

I told Oliver about it that afternoon, once he'd finished helping out Father's men for the day.

'Good idea, miss,' he said. 'Can't hurt to look.'

Oliver helped me search, although I knew that he couldn't read any of Father's cursive writing. Nevertheless, I was glad not to be alone. It didn't take long for me to find the ledger where Father had recorded all those we'd employed. I heaved it on to the desk with a thud, and a small cloud of dust came out.

As I flipped through, I saw that it had all sorts of detail about the household accounts and who was paid what. Father, who was always organised, had kept a list of the servants' names in the back.

I ran my finger down the names. 'Too young. Too young. Too *old* . . .'

Oliver hovered nearby nervously, and Bones was doing the same, his tail flicking as his eyes darted back and forth between the both of us. 'Are we looking for the Black Widow?'

'I *think* so,' I said. 'It's all we have to go on. If she dropped those mysterious notes . . .'

Those had been playing on my mind. Especially the fact that she seemed to be spreading rumours. She could well have been accusing Father.

He wrung his hands. 'What if it's not her? Or what if she has an accomplice?'

I shot him a look. 'That might be, but you're just complicating matters.' Truth be told, the notion that we were on completely the wrong track had occurred to me, and it was terrifying. We were Father's only hope. The detective inspector didn't look like he was interested in running after other leads when he had a perfectly good scapegoat locked up in a cell. 'It has to be her.' I paused. 'Though I have to admit, I don't remember any of our servants having a scarred face.'

'Scars can happen any time,' Oliver said, rubbing his head. I caught a glimpse of the red welt under his hair. Bones nuzzled his leg sympathetically. 'And it don't mean a person is bad.'

Seeing Oliver's point, I nodded and carried on looking through the list. 'Hmm,' I said aloud. 'Mrs Jane Barker, our governess. She was about the right age, and she looked fairly similar to what I've glimpsed of the Black Widow . . .'

'She ever act strange?' he asked.

I bit my lip. I wasn't sure. Mrs Barker was *pretty* strange, from what I remembered. She had a glass eye, and when she sang she sounded a bit like a howling dog. If Bones had been there, he would probably have tried to join in. 'Well, she wasn't boring, that was for sure.' Another detail came to mind. 'Ah, but then she walked with a crutch.'

Oliver frowned. 'It can't be her then. The Black Widow seems to hurry along with no trouble.'

'Exactly.' I slipped my finger down to the next name in the list, and that was where I stopped. 'Oh . . .'

'What?' Oliver leaned closer to the desk to peer at the book. Bones looked up, pressing his nose against me.

'This could be it,' I whispered. 'Miss Emily Stone.'

Bones whined suddenly – almost like a howl. My skin broke into goosebumps.

Miss Stone was our other governess. Our first governess, actually. I had been fairly young when she was let go – the first of our servants to leave. So many of them had then left – I didn't think anything of it.

I looked up at Oliver. 'She was thin, pale, light-haired . . . just like the Black Widow. No scar, but – like you say, she might have acquired that.'

'What was she like?' he asked.

I shrugged. 'I barely recall her beyond that.' I tried desperately to search the depths of my memory. 'She was only with us for a short time. I think . . . I think she could be a bit cold and distant, but she taught me well enough.'

'Is that all?' He bent over the ledger, as if it were somehow going to reveal more secrets to him. 'You don't remember anything else that could help?'

I slammed the book shut, making Oliver jump and Bones cower under the desk. 'That's all I have! I was so young, Oliver. What more is there to say?'

He sighed, bent down and started stroking Bones until he stopped quivering. 'All right, miss. I know.'

Now I felt bad. 'It's not you, it's Father, and all this, I just—' My apology was interrupted by a knock on the door of the shop.

With a glance at Oliver I headed to answer, but Bones beat me to it, his tail now wagging hopefully. *He thinks it's Father come home*, I thought, but I didn't have anywhere near such high hopes.

I turned the key in the lock and opened the door. 'Sorry, we're closed—' I started, but a bright flash went off in my face, blinding me, a puff of smoke filling my nose. Bones sprang into a crouch, growling and snapping.

I blinked rapidly and when I could finally see again, I found myself looking up at four men, all wearing peaked caps. Three of them had notebooks, while the fourth stood behind the offending camera that had just struck me senseless. 'I . . . what is this?' I coughed through the acrid smoke.

'Miss Veil?' one of them said. He pointed to himself with his pencil. 'Jim Dean, *Gazette and Herald.* Is it true that your father is in prison for the recent murders?'

I gaped at him.

'Miss Veil,' one of the others said, 'Tempest Smith, *Weekly Bugle*. They're calling him the Undertaker of Death. How do you feel about that name?'

A small crowd of nosy onlookers was forming behind the journalists. I felt my face burn brighter and brighter red. 'Please, leave us alone.'

'No comment, then,' Tempest Smith replied, shaking his head sadly as if I'd let him down. My chest felt tight.

The last of them stepped forward from behind the large tripod that the photographer was using. 'Miss Veil, Jeffery Briar of the *Morning Times* here – will you go to watch your father hang?'

I felt the world begin to spin and blur around me.

'Murderer!' someone cried with enthusiasm from the crowd. 'Vile villain!'

I was aware of Bones leaping forward, nipping the man on his ankle, and suddenly Oliver was beside me, tugging Bones back and grabbing the door. 'No more questions!' he shouted at them. 'Leave us alone!' He pushed me back, and the door closed to another *crack* as the camera flash went off once more.

Like a house of cards, I fell to the floor, piece by piece.

Time was running out . . . I had to get to the bottom of this crime, and quickly . . .

Because the vultures had found us.

Chapter Twenty

Mother came rushing in, with Thomas trailing not far behind. Bones circled the room, growling at the door, while Oliver flattened himself against it.

'What on earth is the matter?' Mother exclaimed from high above me. 'I heard a commotion!'

My head was still spinning, and my mouth flapping uselessly.

'R-reporters, ma'am,' Oliver managed to stammer out. 'Lots of them.'

I looked up at the window. Having had the door shut in

their faces, the reporters and local gossips had swarmed in front of the glass. I could see a line of eyes as they peered in.

Mother's face began to burn red with anger. 'Thomas, shut the curtains!' she ordered. 'Oliver, lock the door!'

They did as they were told, Thomas pulling the black velvet curtains (that were rarely ever drawn, and so released a cloud of dust) across the window and Oliver reluctantly moving from his defensive position to turn the key in the lock.

'Mother,' I said weakly from the floor, keeping my voice quiet so that Thomas wouldn't hear. 'They were saying such horrible things.' I hated sounding like this, but I couldn't hold back the despair.

Mother dropped down beside me, which was not easy in her full skirts. She wrapped her arms round my shoulders. 'Shh, it's all right,' she soothed me. 'Don't listen to them.'

I wanted to tell her what they'd asked, what people had shouted out about Father, but I couldn't bring myself to. I couldn't do it to her. It was awful, truly awful. They all believed Father was a murderer, that he would hang.

For a few moments, I just stared at nothing, feeling emptiness and hopelessness overwhelm me.

Bones ceased his growling, pattered over and began to lick my face. It brought me back to reality with a thud. I rubbed his soft head gently.

Mother sniffed and stood up, offering her arm to help me up too, away from the affections of the dog. 'We shan't use the front door,' she said. 'Not until your father is home. We'll go through the cemetery.'

'Oh, but Mother . . .' Thomas began to protest, wiping his hands on his britches.

She raised a finger at him. 'I mean it, Thomas. This is for your safety. Do as you're told.'

Thomas's lower lip wobbled and his brow narrowed, but he said nothing. I frowned at him.

Mother breathed out sharply. 'Let us all pray that they get tired and leave us alone. Come along.' With one last angry glance towards the window, she left the shop, gesturing at us to follow. Bones trotted after her.

Thomas scuffed his feet on the floor.

'Stop it, Thomas,' I snapped at him. 'This isn't the time to behave like a spoilt child. Mother and Father need us more than ever.'

He continued pouting. Then he said, 'I don't understand! I don't want to have to walk through the cemetery all the time! It takes so much longer to go that way.'

'Well, we're doing it,' I told him. 'For safety. You heard.'

'No one tells me what's going on!' He threw his hands down at his sides, glared at me, and then shuffled out.

I gave an exasperated sigh.

'Is it really safer in the cemetery, though, miss?' Oliver said. I turned to him. 'What with the Black Widow possibly lurking out there . . .'

I put my hand to my mouth. 'The Black Widow! That's what we were talking about!'

I looked back at the open book on the desk and once again my eyes landed on Miss Stone's name. Now that I thought about it, there *had* been something odd about her that I couldn't quite put my finger on. Miss Barker had been eccentric, of course, but I didn't think she had a bad heart. Miss Stone, on the other hand . . . She seemed normal, but . . . what if there was something hidden underneath her quiet demeanour? Even picturing her in my memory made me feel slightly on edge. 'I may not remember her well, but I think Miss Stone needs to be top of our list of suspects for the identity of the Black Widow,' I told Oliver. 'She's the only one who really fits the bill.'

'Seems a possibility. But how do we find out about her? We could try asking at the police station again,' Oliver suggested, with a hopeful expression. He pulled a pencil out from behind his ear that I hadn't even noticed was there.

'Oh, you and your playing Jack Danger!' I said, swatting him on the arm. 'I've had enough of reporters for one day. But . . . yes, that could work, if she's known to them for anything. I don't fancy running into Inspector Holbrook again, though.' I shuddered. 'We need to avoid the press too.' Their horrible words echoed in my mind.

Murderer. Villain. Undertaker of Death.

I tried to pretend I couldn't hear them. I drowned them out with my own words.

Father is innocent. Father is innocent.

We were running out of time. I needed the distraction of investigating.

'Wait,' I said. 'The servants who were here back then may have left, but Alfred the gravedigger has been here for years and years. Maybe he'll remember something about Miss Stone.'

Oliver nodded thoughtfully. 'And if she is the Black Widow, he might have seen her hanging around here like a bad smell.'

I snapped my fingers. 'You're right.' I looked up at the clock. 'He'll be heading home now – but we can catch him first thing tomorrow morning.'

Perhaps the whole world would believe Father's guilt when they read the morning papers. But Oliver and I . . . maybe, just maybe, we could change the world.

The next morning, once I was certain that everyone else was occupied – Maddy helping Mother see to the household chores and Thomas grumpily assembling his toy soldiers – I knew we could sneak out into the cemetery to find Alfred. The others needed to keep busy to distract themselves from what was happening, and I do too. I, however, had different methods.

Bones, of course, insisted on following us. He quickly found his favourite stick hidden behind the lavatory in the garden and padded along beside us.

'Good boy,' I told him, remembering how he'd defended me before. 'If we run into the Black Widow, you can bite her too.' He wagged his tail in what appeared to be happy agreement. I hoped he would get the right person this time, though.

The sky was the colour of milk, the trees like skeletons with a few crispy leaves still clinging on. As I opened the back gate, Bones happily ran out and began dancing through them, sending up spiralling clouds of amber.

Oliver and I peered out, but there didn't seem to be any sign of journalists. The cemetery was peaceful as usual. I breathed a sigh of relief.

We had three gravediggers, and Alfred had been with us the longest. As we walked out that day I could see him taking a rest against a tree, mopping his furrowed brow with his handkerchief. His spade stood upright in the dirt. Even on a chilly day, digging was hot and exhausting work – back-breaking, even. I often wondered how he did it.

Alfred looked up as Bones ran over to him and dashed around his feet in excitement. He leaned down and patted the dog on the head, making a fuss of him. Then he smiled and waved at me, and I waved back, before moving my thumb back and forth across my chest.

Oliver looked at me questioningly.

'He's deaf,' I explained. 'Give me your notebook, would you?'

Whenever I had a moment with Alfred, I would get him to teach me some of his finger signs. Unfortunately, I didn't know enough to ask what we needed to ask. He could read lip movements, but he always said I spoke too fast for him (this was probably true – Mother often told me I could speak at a mile a minute). Unlike Oliver, he was a keen reader, so he'd always ask me to write things down instead.

Oliver offered his notebook and pencil from his pocket. I took it and hastily scribbled a question as we walked over, crunching through the leaves. I handed it to Alfred, who peered down at it.

'Oh,' he said, blinking. 'Miss Stone? Yes, I remember her. Strange woman. She used to sit and watch me digging sometimes, but she would never say a word to me. Gave me an odd feeling.'

I turned over the page and scribbled again. *Did she get sacked? Did you know anything else about her?*

'Scratched?' He squinted at the words on the page.

Oops – my messy handwriting. I rewrote the word and tapped it with the pencil.

'Oh, sacked?' Alfred read. 'Perhaps. I didn't know her, and as I say she never tried to speak to me. I think she lived not far from here, because she was often walking through. Could be she was sacked . . . The last day I saw her, she looked tearful.'

That would make sense with what Maddy had said. Miss Stone certainly wouldn't have been happy. I added another note. *Have you seen her recently? In the cemetery?*

He shook his head. 'I don't . . . think so, Miss Violet. Not for years.'

I frowned. He hadn't seen her? But we knew the Black Widow had been here, and I had felt a growing certainty they were one and the same.

Oliver had his hands in his pockets and was shuffling from foot to foot, looking around nervously. I wasn't sure if it was Miss Stone or the journalists that he was worried about. 'If the lady looks different though, miss?'

Bones barked as if in agreement. 'Hmm,' I said to myself.

I wrote a final question and handed it to Alfred. *Have you seen a strange lady in black, with a veiled face and a scar?*

He stared down at this one for a few moments before answering. 'Well, miss, every other woman around here is dressed in mourning clothes, you know. I don't know if I've seen this one you're looking for, but . . .'

I motioned to him to give back the notebook and then added – *around plot 239?*

Alfred had an encyclopaedic knowledge of the layout of the graves and tombs. I felt sure he would know what I was talking about.

'Ah,' he said, scratching his beard. 'There was a lady like that up there today. Not so long ago. You looking for her? She might still be there . . .'

I shared a glance with Oliver, who was wide-eyed. He took his notebook back from Alfred and I hastily signed *Thank you, thank you!* as we ran away up the hill, Bones shooting ahead of us like he was chasing rabbits.

CHAPTER TWENTY-ONE

There was a tomb in the cemetery, one of the very oldest, that I knew well. It belonged to a Mrs Sarah Bailey. We passed close by it as we ran, Bones somehow knowing exactly where to go as he always did.

It had a poem engraved on it, a little faded now from years of wear. I'd first read it as a young child, clinging to my mother's hand.

Mortality behold and fear
What a change of flesh is here
In this tomb lieth a mother
And eight of her children with her

I remembered Mother shuddering as I read it aloud, stumbling over each word. 'A horrible thought,' she'd said. Even as someone who took death in her stride daily, the message made her deeply sad.

I could feel the sadness of it too, but that wasn't all. There was a deep love as well. A distant echo of laughter, and the smell of apple pie on the wind. The stone under my fingers felt soft and silky, like my mother's dresses. I didn't know then that only I could feel those things.

The words had always stuck in my mind. I remembered asking Mrs Barker the governess about it, much later.

'*Memento mori*,' she'd replied.

'What?' I'd asked, screwing up my face in confusion.

'It's a Latin phrase,' she said. 'It means "remember death", or perhaps "remember you will die". You will see many reminders of death around a graveyard.'

I thought to myself that I wasn't likely to forget it, what with an undertaker for a father, but I still didn't understand. 'Why do they want to remind people of that? Do they want them to be sad?'

'Oh no,' said Mrs Barker. 'I don't believe so. I believe it's a call to live a better life. To do what you can with the time you have.'

As we hurried past the tomb, I reached out and ran my fingers over the words, the soft feeling tickling my fingertips. What Mrs Barker had said had always stuck with me. It wasn't scary to remember I would die, not for me. It was exhilarating. It meant that right now, in this moment, I was alive. I could do anything. It was now or never.

But as we turned a corner of the path and I saw what I hoped for but what I was also dreading – the Black Widow was walking the path ahead of us – I prayed my death wasn't about to come sooner than expected.

I shoved Oliver behind a tall column. 'Stay here,' I hissed. He was about to protest, but I pointed Bones towards him. 'Bones, make him stay,' I ordered.

Bones was nothing if not obedient, and he gave a low growl at Oliver when he tried to move.

'All right, all right,' Oliver whispered back.

It was for his own safety. If the Black Widow knew he wasn't dead, she might want to change that – but I had to take the chance to talk. All I could think of was proving Father innocent.

I steeled myself as I walked towards her. She had paused, fixing the spider brooch in her hair as she read the inscription on a stone angel with broken wings.

Memento mori, the angel seemed to whisper to me. *Now or never.*

'Miss Stone?' I tried.

The Black Widow peeled back the lace from her eyes, and the look she gave me made me think that she hadn't heard the name in a long time.

Now that I was seeing her face to face, in daylight, I knew that I did recognise her. She was older and she had that scar, and her hair seemed to have dulled. Yet I knew deep down that she must be the woman who had once been my governess. Her eyes had that sharpness to them. She was searching my face, and I got the feeling she was wondering whether or not to respond.

'Young Miss Violet?' she eventually replied. Her voice sounded a little croaky, as if from lack of use, yet it had a sweet and light tone to it. Was it false? You catch more flies with honey, after all.

'Yes,' I replied, stepping closer to her with the utmost care. I felt as though I were a tamer approaching a lion that hadn't been fed for some time. 'You remember me?'

Miss Stone smiled. Her smile was pleasant, which threw me off-guard a little. I'd expected a horrible sneer.

She was really rather pretty, in a strange way, but with a coldness of expression that reminded me of an icy December morning. 'Oh yes,' she said. 'I taught you your lessons for a while, did I not? Are you well?'

'Quite well, miss,' I answered, with the briefest of glances backward to make sure that Oliver wasn't visible.

'And your brother?'

'He's well too.' I wasn't sure how I'd expected the day to be going, but exchanging pleasantries with a possible murderer definitely hadn't been on my list of plans.

'Wonderful,' she said. 'Do give my regards to your family.' Then she made a show of pulling out a dainty pocket watch, the face cracked with age. 'Is that the time? I should . . .'

I couldn't let her get away. I needed something to make her stay. 'Have you heard about my father, miss?'

She froze completely for a moment, as if the watch in her hand had stopped time.

'He's been arrested,' I continued. 'Someone's accused him of murder.'

Miss Stone glanced around the cemetery and I thought that she might be about to run. Instead, she moved towards me. I gulped quietly.

'*No*,' she exclaimed. 'How awful. Do you know who that someone might be?'

She tilted her head to one side. I shook mine in response. My pulse was racing.

'You don't think perhaps that he is guilty?' she asked.

'No,' I said firmly, trying to keep the shake from my voice. 'He's innocent.'

'And how do you know that, my dear girl?' Her voice had lost its pleasant tone and gone cold.

Suddenly Bones rushed towards my feet, snapping and growling, his eyes fixed on the governess. I grabbed his collar to hold him, straining as he pulled with all his weight.

Miss Stone took a few steps back in surprise, her own eyes wide as saucers. 'Oh my,' she said. 'I must be going.'

I turned round to see Oliver, who had jumped out from his hiding place.

The two of them stood on the cemetery path. Not moving. Barely blinking.

'*Oh . . .*' gasped Miss Stone under her breath.

Then she turned and hurried away, slipping through the dark trees, black lace streaming out behind her.

I'd been tempted to let Bones run after her, but – and I hated to admit it – I was too afraid. I didn't want to catch up with the Black Widow at that moment. Nor did I want to give her a chance to do something bad to my dog. He was still growling after her, his teeth bared.

Perhaps it was an overreaction – after all, she hadn't really done anything to me. But Bones seemed to sense that something was wrong. And perhaps I shouldn't have told him he could bite her.

I swallowed, and turned back to Oliver. He was white as a sheet. 'Did you see how she reacted when she saw you? She was shocked – as though she wasn't expecting to see you alive!'

There was a moment of silence, only the leaves rustling overhead. And then Oliver finally spoke. 'I don't understand though, miss. I don't recognise her. I don't feel anything.'

'But I'm sure she recognised you!' I insisted, holding tightly to Bones's collar as he strained.

He raised his hands. 'Then why can't I remember?'

'You don't remember anything surrounding your injury,' I reminded him, although I didn't think he needed reminding.

'I remember everything before that. An' I don't remember ever meeting this lady in my life. If she tried to kill me, she must know me, mustn't she? Doesn't there have to be a *reason*?' He rubbed the scar on the back of his head again.

'Not necessarily,' I said, although he was putting some doubt in my mind. Miss Stone had been my governess, and it seemed that perhaps she did have something against

Father from the way she had spoken. Perhaps enough to want to falsely accuse him. If the rumours were true that he'd sacked her, she could be holding a grudge.

But how could she possibly have known Oliver? He wasn't far from being a street urchin. And the other men who had been victims – did she know them too? Nothing really stacked up.

Bones suddenly stopped pulling against me, so I let go of his collar. He looked up at me and then began trotting back. *Hmm.* I supposed we might as well follow.

Oliver stared in the direction that Miss Stone had gone, and then shook his head. 'I just don't understand,' he said again.

'Mother always says life is not for us to understand,' I told him vaguely as I walked past, and he turned to follow me. My mind was elsewhere.

★ ★ ★

Unfortunately, when we reached home, things had taken a turn for the worse.

Mother was sitting at the table, her head in her hands.

'Mother?' I asked as we walked in. Bones ran over and tried to lick her face, but she didn't even react.

Eventually she looked up, and I saw that her cheeks were tear-stained. 'I couldn't stop them,' she said.

'Who?' Oliver asked, but I was already running for the front of the house, to the shop.

The place was chaos.

The police were in there, and they were going through all of our files. They had tossed many of them to the floor. Bones skidded into the room, pushing the papers aside, and growled at the policemen. He ran forward and got one of them by the trousers.

'Get that mutt out of here,' the constable said, trying to shake Bones away from his leg.

'Bones, come here.' I turned to the police. 'What are you doing?' I demanded, but they ignored me.

'No files that match,' one of them said, pointing to the John Doe section. 'He's covered his tracks good.'

Oliver peered in over my shoulder as Bones slunk back behind us.

That was when I saw the detective inspector. He was leaning over Father's desk. I marched right up to him.

'These are Father's things,' I began. 'You have no right—'

Inspector Holbrook swung round and leaned over me. I breathed in sharply. I'd forgotten he was so tall.

His eyes narrowed. 'Has no one ever taught you your place, child?'

My heart quivered between my lungs, but I stood

firm. 'My place is here, sir, and you and your friends are ransacking it!'

The inspector stood staring down at me. It was like he was looking into my soul. Or perhaps he was just trying to decide whether or not to send me packing. 'You're a strange one,' he said finally. 'I'm telling you now, this doesn't concern you.'

He pushed me out of the way with a firm hand and then walked out from behind the desk. Oliver stayed silently fuming in the doorway, but I had noticed something. The inspector had made a big mistake – he hadn't put away the papers he had been looking at.

I snatched one up.

Edgar D. Veil

You owe us and your time is up

You must meet our demands and

remove the first target – do this now

or your family will pay the price.

My jaw dropped.

Someone had been blackmailing Father. And worse, it sounded like they wanted him to do something bad. *Very* bad.

And now I was left with the question – had he done as they said?

Chapter Twenty-Two

I couldn't stop staring at the letter, my eyes glued to it as if it were flypaper. The words swam in my vision. Whatever had my father got himself involved with?

'What is it?' Oliver hissed in my ear.

I turned to him, certain I must look a fright. His expression became one of concern when he saw my face.

'Blackmail,' I whispered back, waving the letter. 'Someone threatened Father. It sounds like they wanted him to . . . hurt somebody.'

Oliver looked sickened. 'No,' he said.

That 'no' echoed in my mind.

No. No. No.

I slapped the letter down on the desk.

'No!' I called out.

Inspector Holbrook turned round and looked at me. The other policemen stopped and stared. Bones whimpered.

'No,' I said again. I was shaking. 'This isn't true. This letter is a fake.'

The inspector raised an eyebrow at me. 'What makes you say that?'

'It's typewritten,' I told him, 'and not signed. Anyone could have written this!'

'Look, girl—' he began with a wave of a huge hand.

'Violet,' I corrected.

He barely blinked. 'Listen here. Your father has got himself involved with bad people. He has dangerous debts . . .'

'No, he doesn't,' I insisted. I felt sure I would know about such a thing. 'We may have had to cut a few corners lately, but we aren't in financial difficulties.'

One of the policemen laughed at that, and I felt my cheeks burning. How dare they?

'Just look at this place,' the other policeman said.

What was he talking about? I glanced around the shop. It was a little dusty, perhaps, and some things were looking a bit worse for wear. There were some cobwebs springing up. But that was just because we were down to only one servant, wasn't it? We'd just had to let a lot of the servants go because . . .

Because . . .

Oh no.

Doubt started to hit me, then. It wasn't just a matter of 'cutting corners', was it? Things *were* bad. How could I have missed it? I was so caught up in myself that I hadn't noticed the trouble we were in.

If Father really had debts to the wrong people . . . then perhaps they could have threatened him. Told him to do these terrible things. He wouldn't . . . would he? Though if it were to protect us . . .

The policeman who'd laughed must have noticed the change in my expression, because now he was looking smug. 'You'd think business would be booming in an undertaker's in this day and age, wouldn't you?'

'Too right,' the other one replied.

The inspector turned to them. 'Quiet,' he said, and both immediately went silent and turned back to rifling through our files. 'Young miss, you may want to believe your father is innocent.' His tone seemed sympathetic, but his expression was so cold and hard that no kindness shone through. 'But you are wrong.'

Bones growled up at him. I frowned, feeling hot and shaky. Bones didn't trust these constables, so I didn't either.

'We know what we're doing,' the inspector continued. 'Your father was in deep debt to people from the wrong side of town. We have proof –' he pointed to the letter lying on the desk – 'that they told him to commit these crimes. They gave him the four victims' names.'

He held up a sheet of paper briefly – and I caught a glimpse of the names, but none of them were Oliver's.

'And as you know, we found the murder weapon right here in your home,' he finished.

'But—' I tried. It couldn't be.

'No buts,' he snapped. 'Your father is guilty. We almost have all the evidence we need, and he will hang.'

I tried to scream a protest, but it got stuck in my throat. I thought my heart would fall out of my chest, but somehow words were failing me. Doubt had wormed its way in.

'*You're* wrong,' Oliver suddenly said. 'He's innocent.'

I think both the inspector and I were surprised that he had spoken.

'And who are you, boy?' Inspector Holbrook asked him.

I gave a quick shake of my head – worried that Oliver

might start explaining precisely who he was and why he was in our house. They might think it suspicious. And since Oliver couldn't remember his attacker, I felt sure the police would take anything he said as yet more proof that Father was the murderer. Besides, we couldn't risk it threatening our investigation.

'Mr Veil took me in,' Oliver said. I could hear the quiet rage in his voice. 'He saved me from the workhouse. He's a good man, and he would never do this. I don't care what the note says. You're wrong.'

I squeezed my fingers together, focused on my breathing. I had to listen to Oliver. Father wouldn't help him if he'd been the one to try to kill him, would he?

But he feels guilty . . . a treacherous voice whispered inside my mind. I shook the thought away.

I heard another small chuckle from one of the policemen. I wanted to hit him. How could they be so sure of themselves?

Unless . . .

Unless this was all part of someone's plan.

Of course. Someone was plotting this. They had to be. This anonymous threat could have been typed by anyone. There was no proof that my father had even seen it. And why hadn't we spotted it before, if it had really been there?

And Inspector Holbrook and his constables seemed

awfully set on Father's guilt. They laughed at him while he faced a terrible fate. To top it all off, Bones was clearly sensing something bad about them.

Finally my words spilled out.

'Why are you doing this?' I demanded. 'Why are you pinning the blame on my father? Have you something against him?'

I was poised to fight, but the inspector just looked at me with incredulity. 'Get her out of here,' he said.

'What—' I started, but suddenly one of the constables was in front of me.

'Out,' he said.

Oliver stared up at him. 'No, we—'

'Both of you,' the constable said. 'And the mutt.' He started walking forward, cornering us. Bones whimpered and darted back out into the corridor. We had no choice. We shuffled backwards, and the policeman slammed the door in our faces.

* * *

'They're corrupt,' I insisted, as I nursed a cup of hot tea in our kitchen. 'Someone must be paying them off, or, or . . . Or they're enemies of Father.' I was trying to convince myself more than anything. There had to be an explanation. Anything other than Father's guilt.

'I'm not sure about them coppers neither,' Oliver said, shaking his head in sad agreement.

Maddy forced a cup of tea into my mother's hands. Mother barely looked up. 'They're the police,' she said in a shaky voice. 'Surely they know what's right and wrong . . .'

'I wouldn't be so sure, ma'am,' Maddy muttered.

'They do know,' I insisted. 'They know they're setting him up. Or that they don't have the evidence right, at least! They must do!' Bones whined at my feet and I took it as his agreement – but perhaps he just wanted a biscuit. 'The way they're acting is just completely wrong. And their "evidence" is flimsy. They won't accept that it could have easily been planted.'

Mother sighed. Her teacup trembled in her hands, a small drop spilling on to the saucer. She turned to my brother. 'Thomas? Go and play outside,' she said. For once, he didn't argue, shuffling out of the back door with his hands wedged in the pockets of his britches.

It was horrible to see my mother in this state. But I knew that what I had to tell her was going to make things much worse.

'Mother, they . . . They have these awful letters. I have no idea where they found them, because we searched the whole office just the other day, which makes it all the more suspicious in my opinion, but anyway, they—'

Mother's gaze suddenly snapped to mine. 'What letters, Violet?'

I took a deep breath. 'Blackmail. Father was being blackmailed.'

I heard a gasp and the tinkling sound of Maddy dropping a spoon in the sink. I turned to her, but she flushed red and hurried away out of the kitchen. I think she felt she'd heard too much.

Oliver looked the same – he was shifting uncomfortably in his seat, and his expression said he'd rather be anywhere else. Bones went over and put his nose in his lap.

'What sort of blackmail?' Mother asked, her voice flat and lifeless as if she already knew what I was going to say.

'It said he owed someone and that they would hurt us if he didn't do as they said. And the police said . . .' I winced. 'They said he was told to kill all those men. Because he had dangerous debts.'

I hadn't thought it possible, but the colour drained out of Mother's face even further. She looked as if she were about to be sick. Oliver was just staring down at the table.

'But it's not true, is it?' I asked desperately. 'Father doesn't owe money to bad people? I know we haven't been doing so well recently, but—'

'ENOUGH.' Mother stood up so suddenly that the table shook, spilling the tea everywhere. My breath caught in my throat and Oliver flinched. 'We will not speak of this any further.' There were tears in her eyes.

'Mother, I . . .' I started, but she just shook her head and left. Bones ran out after her.

Now I began to feel sick. Mother's reaction had spoken more than words. So the part about Father's awful debts was true – or at least Mother suspected it was.

'This is bad,' I said quietly to Oliver. He nodded his agreement.

'But – but it still doesn't mean anything.' I slammed my hand down on the table, sending the spilled tea jumping. 'The police could have known about the debts and forged the blackmail letters! Or . . .'

'Or the letters are real,' Oliver finished. 'But that don't mean your pa did any of what they wanted.'

'He wouldn't,' I agreed. I tried to put the certainty into my words that wouldn't come to my mind. Then something occurred to me. 'They didn't have your name though, did they?'

'I don't know, miss,' said Oliver, his brow drawn. 'What did you see?'

I closed my eyes, trying to remember. 'I only caught sight of the list for a second, but I'm sure I didn't see your name on there. And he only mentioned four victims. We know there were five if we include you.'

'What do you think it means?'

'Hmm.' I wrinkled my brow. 'It could be a clue that Father has been falsely accused – because whoever did this didn't know about you. Or if they did, they didn't know your name!'

'Or they know I'm alive,' he pointed out. 'An' they don't want to send the bobbies looking for me.'

Hmm. It was all adding up . . . to something. But what it was, I couldn't be sure. This whole thing was getting stranger and stranger. If only we could work out what connected the victims . . . It all just felt so hopeless. If even I was beginning to question my father's innocence, he stood no chance in front of a judge.

I got up to fetch a cloth, and dried the remains of Mother's tea from the table. I did hope she would be all right. Without Father, we needed her to hold the family together.

Just then, I heard a scrabble of paws on the kitchen floor and looked round to see Bones coming back in. He had something in his mouth. He padded over and dropped it into my lap.

It was the piece of paper with the list of victims' names.

I grinned down at Bones. 'Well done, boy,' I said. Now we could investigate the list ourselves. Perhaps there was hope yet!

Chapter Twenty-Three

There were four names on the list:

Randall Wutherford
Bjorn Wulf Eriksen
Joseph Comely-Parsons
Winston Aberforth

None were names that I recognised, but I had to say they all had a fancy ring to them. They didn't sound like the names of your average man on the street, or the penniless man in the workhouse. Yet somehow these relatively young men had all ended up in our cemetery, in paupers' graves with no headstones. Only the generosity of my father had seen to it that they had separate graves at all. No one had identified them – until now.

Whatever game Inspector Holbrook was playing, I felt certain he would have let the victims' families know about their deaths. Which raised the question – what had they believed had become of these men before now? That they had gone missing? Or – a darker thought – did they not care?

There were answers out there somewhere, and Oliver and I needed to find them. That was what I had to focus on. I tried to put Father's debts out of my mind for now. Being in debt didn't make him guilty of murder, I knew that much. If the blackmail was real, though . . . I shivered. Our lives could really be at stake, and Father – to what lengths would he have gone to protect us?

Unfortunately, the letter gave us nothing to go on as to who could have sent it or forged it. The list of names at least gave us a place to start, though, and I thought I had a plan for how to do it.

'But how will we find these people?' Oliver asked. 'We can't exactly get Bones to sniff 'em out, not when they're . . . you know.'

'Dead?' I replied, setting the paper back down on the table. 'Precisely. But they must have families. And they aren't *long* dead.'

Oliver still looked puzzled. 'So we ask around? The *whole* city?'

I stared at him. 'No, you silly goose. There's a much easier way. Come on.'

* * *

I could hear Maddy consoling Mother somewhere inside the house.

'We're just going out to the cemetery!' I called.

Maddy's head appeared round a doorframe. 'No further, all right, young miss?'

'Of course,' I said, my fingers firmly crossed behind my back.

I knew I was misbehaving. Frankly, with all that had happened the past couple of days, I thought that most people would be lying in bed with a cold compress over their eyes at this point. I, however, was not about to give up. If I had to misbehave, then so be it. We'd be back before they had a chance to wonder where we'd gone.

With the list of names firmly grasped in my gloved hand, I followed Bones and Oliver outside. Bones darted off ahead of us.

Our destination was the Post Office, which seemed to perplex Oliver somewhat.

'We can't send letters to dead folks, miss,' he said. 'What good would that do?'

I just laughed. He would soon see what I was up to.

The Post Office was merely a few streets away once we'd exited the cemetery through the tall iron gates. We ran to keep up with Bones and stopped outside to catch our breath, blowing misty clouds into the chilly air.

Bones whined and pawed at the ground. I looked up to see a sign on the door that read

NO DOGS ALLOWED

Spoilsports.

'Stay here and look after him,' I said, and I was pretty certain that both Oliver and Bones each thought I was speaking to them.

When I came back outside a short while later, Oliver was sitting on the pavement, scratching Bones behind the ears. They both jumped up to greet me. 'Well?' Oliver said. 'Did you find anything?'

I held out the piece of paper, which now had lines of my messy looped handwriting below each name.

Randall Wutherford
8 Barnaby Crescent

Bjorn Wulf Eriksen
15 Pleasantview, Lansdowne

Joseph Comely-Parsons
Windermere House, Jeffords Lane

Winston Aberforth
Arnvale House, Coppington Avenue

'Addresses,' I explained, tapping them. 'The Post Office directory has almost everyone in the city. Or at least anyone who is head of a household.' That unfortunately meant I'd have no chance of looking up the whereabouts of Miss Stone – not to mention that her name was so common. 'All of these men were in there. I suppose it hasn't yet been updated since their untimely demise.'

Oliver nodded thoughtfully. 'Clever. So all of them are heads of a household? Rich blokes?'

'Good thinking,' I replied. 'I thought perhaps so from the names, but this does seem to confirm it. Let's go!'

'Whoa, whoa!' Oliver held out his hands and stopped me from marching away. 'You want to go to these places now? Shouldn't we be getting back?'

Bones looked up at me, his head tilted to one side as if he was questioning my decisions as well.

'No time like the present,' I said, eagerly gripping my list as a gust of wind threatened to grab it.

'It's not really the time—' Oliver started, with an anxious glance back down the street.

'There is *no time*!' I shot back. My tone was perhaps a little harsher than I had intended. 'Or did you forget that my father is locked up and waiting for the hangman?'

Oliver said nothing for a moment, his big brown eyes just staring back at me. Then he finally continued: 'He wouldn't want anything to happen to you, miss. An' I don't neither.'

'Then come with me,' I said. I waved the paper at him. 'I know Coppington Avenue – it's a five-minute walk away. If it'll make you feel better, we can head straight home afterwards.' To be quite honest, I wasn't sure where the others were, and would need to look them up on a map anyway. But I hoped Oliver would feel as though he were getting a compromise.

He breathed out a small sigh. 'All right. Let's go.'

Bones gave a cheerful bark and wagged his tail. 'Go on then, boy!' I told him. 'Lead the way!'

Coppington Avenue was one of the fanciest streets in our surrounding area. It was lined with poplar trees that shaded the grand stone dwellings, many with their own driveways and coach houses. Unlike many of the nearby roads that were dirty and shabby, the residents seemed to have made the effort to keep everything well swept.

A pair of ladies covered in jewellery walked past us arm in arm, their long skirts sweeping the pavement.

Oliver whistled through his teeth as we turned the corner. 'Toffs,' he said.

'Indeed,' I replied. 'If Mr Aberforth owned a house here, he was a very rich man.'

Bones trotted ahead of us and came to a stop outside a large pair of wrought-iron gates. He sniffed along the bottom of it, looking a bit unhappy. The sign read:

Arnvale House

I followed him and tried the gates. 'Blast,' I said. 'Locked.' I peered inside at the house up ahead. All seemed quiet, and the windows were covered with black drapes. The house was in mourning. I scuffed my shoe against the pavement. 'We're stuck.'

'Wait, Bones,' Oliver said suddenly, and I turned to see Bones dashing up the pavement and into a gap in the wall.

With a quick glance at each other, Oliver and I ran after him and came to another, much smaller gate. This one was wide open, and led to a little path that snaked its way round the back. The servants' entrance, surely.

'Bones!' I called. I spotted a black nose poking out from behind the back wall of the house. 'Come here!'

His face stuck out a little further, but he didn't move. He wanted us to follow him.

I took a deep breath and picked up my skirts. 'All right . . .'

'Miss,' said Oliver, shuffling his feet. 'They might . . . shoot us or something if we trespass.'

'Oh, come on! This is our lead,' I told him in no uncertain terms. 'We're taking it. If we can find a servant, they might know something.' With that, I stepped on to the path, and followed the wagging tail disappearing from view. I heard reluctant footsteps crunching along the gravel behind me as Oliver followed.

Arnvale House's garden was breathtaking. It had been beautifully landscaped with fountains, statues and splashes of bright flowers everywhere. Yet it was strangely quiet. The water in the fountains remained still, and I couldn't hear any birds singing in the trees. It was as if the whole garden was holding its breath while it waited for news of its master.

I stopped for a second by one of the fountains, trying to feel for any ghostly echoes. All was quiet and still, but I tasted something sour in my mouth.

I turned the corner with the path as it weaved behind the building, through a fragrant patch of herbs and lavender. There was a greenhouse there, brick-built at the bottom and shiny white wood and glass for the top. The door was wide open, and just as I was about to approach it, Bones came trotting into view, pursued rather slowly by an ageing gardener.

'Where did you come from, eh?' he was asking Bones, waving a trowel at him. Bones stopped in front of me and wagged his tail.

My feet felt glued to the spot. Belatedly, I realised I was perhaps being foolish. What on earth was I going to say? How was I going to explain what we were doing there?

The old man's eyes met mine. 'Hullo, young miss,' he said, tipping his flat cap at me. 'Oh, and young master,' he added as Oliver came to a stop beside me.

I breathed out. The gardener seemed friendly enough. Perhaps this would work after all. I just prayed Bones wouldn't start digging up his carrots.

'Good afternoon,' I said. 'I . . . um . . . I'm Violet . . .' I trailed off. I had been about to give my surname, but perhaps that wasn't wise on an investigation. Besides, he might have read the papers. A pseudonym would have been a better idea.

'An' I'm Jack Danger,' said Oliver cheerily. He was clearly a little further ahead of me on that point.

'Can I help you both?' asked the gardener, bending down to stick the trowel into the soil. I noticed his hands were scarred and calloused. Bones tried to lick his fingers. The man smiled and patted him gently.

I gathered myself and tried again. 'We live nearby,' I told him, which wasn't exactly untrue. 'We heard something happened to Mr Aberforth.'

I was expecting the gardener's expression to change – for him to look sad, or angry. They had presumably just had the news that their master had been murdered, after all. But the smile didn't leave his face.

'Oh yes,' he said. He looked almost serene.

I was thrown. 'I'm sorry . . . did you not . . .?'

'Well, between you and me . . .' He tapped his nose at us. 'We won't miss him.'

'But . . . all this?' Oliver said, gesturing at the black-draped windows.

'Pssh,' said the gardener. 'Just for show.' He paused for a moment, looking down at the neat plants. 'Mr Aberforth wasn't a kind man, you see. We all breathed a sigh of relief when he went missing.' He waved his hand slowly in front of me. 'These scars aren't from gardening, lass. One step out of line and he'd beat us over the knuckles with his cane.'

I winced. 'I'm sorry.'

The man simply sighed and looked up at the setting sun, shading his eyes.

'Can you think of anyone who might've wanted your master dead?' Oliver asked.

The gardener looked back at us. 'Anyone,' he said finally. 'Anyone who met him.'

Chapter Twenty-Four

We weaved through the curving paths of the cemetery and back home, only to find that our absence really hadn't been noted. Mother was locked in her room, wading in her sorrows. Thomas was back to playing with his tin soldiers, but he could tell something wasn't right. He kept asking Maddy about Father every two seconds, and soon was being met with nothing but weary looks.

It seemed as though the first part of our investigation was rather fruitless. All we'd gained was that Mr Aberforth was very nasty, and could have been in anyone's bad books. The gardener had told us he didn't know a Miss Stone, either. We hadn't exactly narrowed anything down.

But I wasn't going to let that stop us. Inspector Holbrook and his men may have been determined to pin the murders on my father, but their determination could not match mine. I had to find the truth, whatever it may be.

I spent the evening poring over the city map with Oliver. Although he couldn't read the street names, he could read the streets. I found the addresses of our remaining three victims, and he quickly traced a route. His memory had blank spots, but the city was still his home and he clearly knew it well. I noted that all of the victims lived fairly near to us.

That night, I dreamed of Father. Of the walls pressing in on his cell until he was trapped between them. I woke to find Bones resting on my bed, holding the list of names in his mouth. He knew how to give me purpose.

Mother seemed a little better at breakfast, but there was no mention of Father, nor of his supposed terrible debts. It worried me that she had known about or at least suspected it – and her reaction to the blackmail news had not been good. She chatted about the weather and how she was sure we'd be opening the doors of the business again soon. She was distracting herself, I knew. I felt as though there was an axe hanging over all of our heads. Politely ignoring it wasn't going to save us.

I repeated the names of the victims over and over in my head. *Randall Wutherford. Bjorn Wulf Eriksen. Joseph Comely-Parsons. Winston Aberforth.* And . . . Oliver? How on earth did he fit into all this? These rich, powerful men, and a street boy?

'Do you even have a surname?' I asked Oliver over the table.

He nearly dropped his bacon. 'Um.' He scratched his ear. 'Oats.'

'Oliver Oats?' I teased. 'Sounds like a horse!'

He laughed. 'Says Violet Veil! You sound like . . . well, like an undertaker's daughter, miss.'

He had a point.

I made excuses to Mother so that we could sneak out once again. This time, I promised, we were just going to buy a loaf of bread. Oliver stood with his hands in his pockets, concealing the list of victims. We didn't need the map, he assured me, because he could remember the way. Together with Bones's nose, I was sure we could sniff out the right addresses.

I had peered through the front curtains, only to find

that there were still a few journalists hanging about. We hadn't taken a look at the day's papers, and nor did I want to. Let them say what they liked about Father. We were going to prove him innocent.

Mr Eriksen of Pleasantview was the first and the furthest away. I thought it best to take the omnibus. Mother never liked them – she preferred a cab, and she would have had a fit if she knew I was taking one alone (or with Oliver, which was probably worse). Unfortunately I only had a few coins left in my purse, and with Father locked up, there was a chance I wouldn't get any more. The omnibus was cheaper, and I would still have just enough to buy the bread.

We stood waiting in the street as smaller carriages rattled past. Eventually Bones raised his nose in the air, and sure enough the omnibus came clattering around the corner. How he could sense it over the city's strong odour of horses and chimney smoke, I had no idea.

'Never been on one of these, miss,' Oliver told me.

'Then how did you get about the city?' I asked.

He looked at me as if I were simple. 'With my feet,' he said.

The omnibus was fairly new, with bench seats and painted sides plastered with advertisements for teas and chocolates. I quickly concealed Bones behind my skirts.

He may have been tall but he was a black dog, after all, so he blended in well.

A lanky conductor in a bowler hat hung off the staircase at the back. He tipped his hat at me as I offered him the coins.

'Where you off to then?' he asked us, a little suspiciously.

'Lansdowne,' I told him. 'Pleasantview.'

He tipped his hat and moved aside to let us on. I was glad he didn't ask for a further explanation, because I didn't particularly want to bring up murder. As soon as he was looking the other way, I ushered Bones up the steps.

Oliver and I followed and sat together, wedged rather uncomfortably on a bench seat. Bones curled round my legs. We gained several more curious looks from other passengers, but I ignored them – and Oliver was too entranced by the ride to notice.

'We're so high up,' he kept saying. 'I feel like I'm eight feet tall! Ain't this fun, miss!'

I nodded, although I wasn't sure he could tell I was nodding because the whole thing was so *bumpy*. The omnibus rattled through the streets, bouncing over the cobbles. *Thankfully it's dry today*, I thought to myself, as I watched the wheels spin through the layers of muck in the road. A cold wind blew in our faces, and I pulled my shawl up to cover my nose anyway.

Lansdowne was a *toff* area too, as Oliver noted. It wasn't somewhere he'd ventured very often. We clambered from the omnibus, Bones wobbling down the stairs and then leaping off to the surprise of the conductor, who waved after him shouting 'Oi!' – but by then we were all running.

It was pretty impossible to keep up with Bones, but the greyhound seemed to be holding back a little so that we could follow. Oliver had a rough idea of where we were going, and it didn't take long before we found Pleasantview. It was a Georgian terrace of huge houses overlooking a park.

'What are we going to say this time?' Oliver asked as we stared up at the bright red door with a shiny brass 15 emblazoned above it. It had a matching brass door knocker in the shape of a wolf, from which hung a black wreath.

'I think the less we say, the better,' I replied. We wanted to learn about the victims, not give ourselves away. If word got out that we were investigating . . . it wouldn't be good.

'Can you feel anything here?'

I closed my eyes and listened. My ears heard the distant bustle of the nearby street, the tweeting of birds in the trees, the laughter of some children running through the park. Below that . . . there was nothing but a strange feeling of unease. I blinked my eyes open again. 'I don't think this place is haunted, but I don't think it's particularly happy either.'

I took a deep breath, climbed the steps and knocked on the door. It was opened almost instantly by a tall blond footman in smartly tailored black clothes. 'Good morning,' he said, with a light hint of a Swedish accent. 'The Eriksens are otherwise engaged, I'm afraid.'

'My name is Elizabeth French,' I told him. 'I live down the street. I was so sorry to hear about Mr Eriksen.'

There was the tiniest flicker of expression in his face, and then it was gone again. 'Of course. We are all deeply saddened by his passing.' He said the line like some sort of automaton at a fairground, ordered to repeat it over and over. There was no emotion there.

I pulled out a handkerchief and dabbed at the corner of my eyes. 'Did he suffer?'

The footman looked back blankly. 'We don't know, miss. It is rather a mystery, what happened to him, I'm afraid. He was presumed missing, and we only recently received the news.'

'It's terrible,' I sobbed, perhaps a little too dramatically.

'Yeeees . . .' the footman replied. He didn't sound convinced. 'It is . . .' His eyes darted around as if he was suddenly concerned about being overheard. 'I shouldn't speak of this any further, miss, apologies. As I said, the Eriksens are engaged. Please do call back another time.'

With a polite nod, he shut the door in my face.

I frowned and hopped back down the steps.

'He's hiding something,' said Oliver. Bones whined in what I assumed was agreement.

'Definitely,' I said.

'Didn't like his master too much, I reckon.'

'Hmm.' So it was possible that both our victims so far were unpopular with the people around them. I supposed that made sense. If the letter that Father had received was real, it meant that these men were involved in dark dealings – or at the very least with the wrong people. 'I don't think we're going to get any more here. Let's head to Jeffords Lane.'

Oliver was more familiar with Jeffords Lane. It wasn't in quite such an affluent area as the other places we'd visited, but it wasn't far off. 'Used to shine shoes down Green Street over there, with the shops,' he said, pointing. 'Lots of blokes in suits an' hats and briefcases. They don't want to be seen without the shiniest of shoes.'

'Do you think you ever met Mr Comely-Parsons?' I asked.

Oliver shrugged. 'How would I know? They didn't

want to speak to me. I was just a shoeshine boy. They'd sit an' read the papers while I did it, that was all. Got kicked a few times.'

'That's awful!' I gasped.

His brow wrinkled. 'Just the way it is round here.'

Windermere House was a fairly new brick-built building that boasted white windows and an elegant set of steps to the front, with its own gas lamps. I was just about to approach the door when it was flung open, and a girl in a maid's uniform came running out sobbing. She nearly ran straight into me, making Bones bark.

'Oh, miss, I'm sorry, miss!' she cried. She took a step back and started trying to dry her tears on her apron.

I shared a worried glance with Oliver. 'It's quite all right,' I reassured her. She reminded me a bit of Maddy.

The girl shook her head. 'It's not!' she sniffed.

'What's happened?' Oliver asked her, politely removing his hat.

'I've – I've been sacked,' she said, sinking down on to the steps. 'The mistress won't even give me a reference. I can't believe it! I should have known!' Her mouth was going at a mile a minute. 'That woman told me this would happen, said it was what they've done to everyone else and they know girls like me are too far from home to get help, but oh my, I had to be foolish. But I *needed* this job and what with the master gone I thought things would get better and . . .'

Bones barked again.

Oliver tilted his head. 'You worked for the Comely-Parsons?'

'Y-yes,' the maid stuttered through her tears.

Alarm bells were ringing in my head. 'What did you say about a woman?'

She sniffed again. Her hair was falling out of its tidy bun and she tried in vain to push it back in. 'A-a lady,' she hiccuped, fumbling with her hairpin. 'She was standing outside here when I came about the job advertisement. She told me I shouldn't work for them.' The maid waved up at Windermere House. 'Said they'd just treat me badly and then sack me. That they do it to all the girls, I . . .' She paused mid-sentence. 'Wait. Who are you?'

'Oh, sorry, we're just . . .' I looked around frantically. I'd been caught off-guard by the crying maid. *Aha* – Oliver's cap. I snatched it from him. 'Collecting for the orphans,' I told her, shaking it a bit. I hoped she wouldn't notice that there weren't even any coins in it.

She blinked away a few more tears. 'Sorry, miss. Barely a penny to me name now, miss.'

I felt awful. In the past I probably would have run home and asked Father if we could hire her, but that was no longer possible. 'Well, there is something you can do for us,' I told her. 'Can you tell us what this lady who spoke to you looked like?'

'She was kind to me,' said the maid, burying her head in her apron so her words came out slightly muffled. 'I should have listened to her. She was right about him.'

That hadn't answered the question, and I was getting desperate. 'But what did she look like?' I asked as gently as I could.

'Oh.' The girl lifted her head again. 'She was all in black. And had a . . .' She dragged a hand slowly down her face.

'A scar,' Oliver said, turning pale.

Miss Stone. The Black Widow.

CHAPTER TWENTY-FIVE

What the housemaid had told us was certainly useful information. It tied Miss Stone to one of the victims. But it didn't completely make sense to me.

'The maid said she was kind to her,' I was saying to Oliver.

He wrinkled his nose. 'I know. Don't really sound like a murderer, do it?'

And how did this fit with the blackmail note? If it were real, and there were some angry creditor out there who wanted these men dead – why would Miss Stone be involved? Perhaps this proved what I hoped – that Father was being falsely accused. He couldn't be guilty.

It all went through my mind as we travelled on the omnibus, bouncing through the streets with Bones once again curled up at my feet and trying not to be noticed.

My purse was now considerably lighter than it had been. I gave the maid a penny for what she had told us – I was expecting her to ask why a charity would *give away* pennies, but she was in too much of a state to question it and just thanked me profusely. Of course I also had to remember that I needed to pick up a loaf of bread before going home – otherwise Mother would realise I had been lying about my whereabouts all day. Then all my money would be gone.

I tried not to think about it. It was temporary. We were going to free Father, and prove that he had nothing to do with all this. I had to believe that.

Barnaby Crescent, the home of Randall Wutherford, was the last stop on our trail. It wasn't that far from the cemetery, just a few streets away. It was another grand street, a Georgian arc of houses with black iron railings and balconies. Stone balustrades at the top hid the servants' quarters from view.

Bones went dashing ahead of us, and stopped right

outside number 8. We ran to keep up with him. He climbed the steps and began sniffing the black front door.

'Bones,' I hissed from the pavement. 'Come back!'

He ignored me, and kept on sniffing and pacing up and down. A low growl began to build in his throat.

'What is it, boy?' Oliver asked, almost as if he expected the dog to answer.

Bones kept growling.

'He didn't act like this at any of the other victims' houses,' I said. 'Something's wrong.' I gripped the cold iron railings and tried to use my other sense, but there was no hint of ghostly activity. No tingle on my fingertips, no whispers in my ears.

With hindsight, we should have paid attention to Bones more quickly. We should have run back the way we came from.

Because the black door of number 8 suddenly swung open, and out marched Inspector Holbrook.

'YOU!' he barked, the second he saw us. There were two other policemen behind him, politely readjusting their helmets. They both narrowed their eyes in our direction.

I gulped. I didn't think we stood a chance of getting away from three policemen. Bones ran back and curled around my legs, whimpering and shaking. He didn't like shouting.

Inspector Holbrook strode over to us and began to

speak, back to his usual manner that remained quiet but felt like it was ordering your soul about. 'You should not be here. What do you think you're doing?'

I was stuck. None of our excuses of being concerned neighbours or collecting for the impoverished were going to work on the inspector. He knew who we were, and he was immediately suspicious. Oliver was just staring at me helplessly, waiting for me to come up with something.

When the moment had gone on a bit too long, I simply had to give the truth. 'We're investigating,' I told him, crossing my arms so tight that I thought I might cut off my circulation.

The condescending look the inspector gave me only emboldened me. *In for a penny, in for a pound*, I thought. 'If you won't do your jobs properly, I shall do them for you.'

One of the men with him laughed. The other leaned back against the railings and began lighting a pipe. They weren't taking me the least bit seriously.

The inspector's look changed to be more quizzical. 'Little girl . . .' He bent down and put his hands on his knees, talking to me as if I were five years old. His watch dangled down in front of me. 'Do you really think that you can save your father by *playing detectives*?'

I felt tears prickling my eyes. 'We're not playing.'

'Then,' he said, 'do you mean for me to take you seriously? In which case I should arrest you for obstructing my investigation, no?'

I could feel the rumble of Bones's growling against my leg, but he was holding back and quivering. Inspector Holbrook frightened him. In all honesty, he frightened me as well. I didn't know what to say.

'Talking to people ain't a crime,' Oliver spoke up from beside me.

'No, no,' said the inspector, shaking his head without breaking eye contact. 'But stealing from a crime scene is.'

'We ain't stolen anything neither!' Oliver insisted. I squeezed the end of his fingertips, feeling warm at his bravery.

'Oh no?' Holbrook said. 'A list of the victims' names went missing. Would you happen to know anything about that?'

'I—' I started.

He held up a warning finger. 'Think very carefully before you answer, young miss. Because of course, if you had nothing to do with it, you would have to explain to me precisely how it is that you are here *investigating* at a victim's house.'

My mind was racing. I had to think of something, but I was fairly certain that he wouldn't like anything I had to say. 'I saw it,' I said eventually. 'I just read the names when you held up the piece of paper.'

The inspector just stared back at me for a moment. 'Then you have an incredible memory and above-average eyesight, is that it?'

I heard a snort from the smoking policeman. Inspector Holbrook was toying with me like a cat with a mouse, and they were most amused. I felt my chest go tight and my lips sealed together.

'Leave her alone,' said Oliver, trying to drag himself up to his full height, though it was little use against the tall inspector. 'You're just a bully!'

Inspector Holbrook barely reacted to him, but I saw a glint in his eyes. 'I'm going to give you a final warning. Stay out of this. I think,' he said, turning to his men, 'that we should take these two down to the station.'

They threw us in the back of a black police wagon, and we protested the entire way to the station – but of course it did no good. The policemen sat at the front and ignored us.

Furious, I slumped down in a heap beside Oliver on the juddering wooden floor. Bones whined at me.

'Don't give me that! You could have bitten them for us this time!' I told him.

Thankfully we weren't officially under arrest. They

simply sat us in a small room in the corner of the station beside the entrance to the jail cells, with a young constable guarding the door. He wore big fluffy sideburns and a bored expression, and was passing his time by reading a newspaper. It was freezing, despite all my layers of clothing. Outside, it had begun to spit with rain. Bones whined and put his head down on his paws.

I shuffled my shoes on the tiled floor, while Oliver stared miserably at the wall. I wondered if there was any chance of getting to see Father again. It was so strange to think that he was down there, somewhere beneath my feet. Trapped behind bars. If only we could see him – perhaps he could tell us something that might help with the investigation. I could ask him about Miss Stone!

Through the open door, I noticed that Pickles and Williams, the two grumpy policemen, were standing not far away. One of them unlocked the prison door as if about to head down there, and said something to the other. Some sort of awful joke at our expense, no doubt. They both laughed.

I suddenly saw an opportunity. I jumped up and leaned out of the room.

'Excuse me, sir,' I said to the constable who was guarding us, as sunnily as I could manage.

He looked up. 'They told me not to talk to you,' he

said, a hint of annoyance in his voice. 'Just got to keep watch until you get collected.'

'I know, I know,' I replied. Oliver gave me a wary look, but I knew what I was doing. 'They've sent you to play nursemaid to us children. They ought to pay you more respect.'

'Huh!' he said, folding the newspaper and slapping it down beside him. 'You've got that right!'

'The inspector didn't even take you along to Barnaby Crescent today,' I said. Oliver wouldn't meet my eye now. He knew I was up to something. 'To investigate Mr Wutherford's murder. He took those other two instead.'

The young constable snorted. 'Pickles and Williams. What a joke! Those two are more interested in smoking their pipes than in proper investigating.'

'Hmm,' I said. 'I thought I heard them saying they were the best police constables in the city.'

He sat up straighter and glared at the two men, but they both carried on laughing and jabbing each other. 'Oh did they now?'

'What was it they called the rest of them, Oliver?' I asked pointedly. 'A bunch of clowns, perhaps?'

He called out, beckoning Pickles and Williams over. 'Think something's funny, do you?'

'Well, your sideburns don't half give me a laugh, Jones,' Williams sneered.

Jones took a deep breath, and I knew for a fact that he was about to launch into a tirade at the other two. The other thing I knew was that, suddenly, none of the eyes in the room were on us. We had minutes, at most.

'I've had it with you two!' I heard him begin. 'You smug know-alls with your . . .'

As he ranted, I grabbed Oliver's arm. Before my friend even had a chance to protest, I tugged him up and out of the room, and ran through the door to the jail cells, Bones slinking after us.

Chapter Twenty-Six

Of all the people that Father had been expecting to see at the door to his cell, I think we were the last he would have imagined.

'Miss, what are you—' Oliver panted as we hurried down the stone steps.

'We have to speak to Father!' I said. 'They're going to realise we're gone soon!'

We stood in the semi-darkness on the cold stone floor, and I knocked quickly on the heavy wood, praying he hadn't been moved. There was a wooden sliding panel that could be opened from our side, so I drew it back. 'Father, it's me!' I hissed.

'Violet?' My father's pale and unshaven face appeared. 'What on earth are you—' He peered around. 'Is that Oliver? And the dog?' Bones had jumped up and was attempting to lick Father's face through the hole in the door.

'No time to explain,' I said, as Oliver gave an awkward little wave. 'I-I . . .' I was suddenly hit with all the emotions that I'd been bottling up, and tears stung at my eyes. 'I'm so sorry. I miss you.' I gulped. 'We're doing what we can to get you out of here. You've been falsely accused, Father! You don't deserve this, whatever the police say!'

'And what do they say?' he asked gently.

I wiped my tears with my handkerchief, but I could still feel more threatening to spill. 'They – they found a blackmail letter,' I told him. 'They believe you were told to kill the victims, and that if you didn't they would hurt us.'

'Blackmail,' he said, without a trace of emotion in his voice.

'Because you have terrible debts,' I said, quiet and ashamed.

'Ah,' he said.

He didn't deny it. It must be true.

I looked up and saw a deep furrow in his brow, his eyes filled with sadness and confusion. 'But . . . a letter, you say? I didn't know about this.'

'You didn't read it?' Oliver asked him.

Father shook his head. 'I don't recall any letter. Perhaps I didn't notice. But . . . This Inspector Holbrook,' he said. 'I think perhaps he has something against me. I don't know what, but in my few interactions with him he has treated me with considerable disdain. Maybe this letter is a forgery.'

'That's what we were wondering!' I exclaimed. 'It was typewritten, Father. It could have been from anyone. Don't you think it's possible that the police could have written it themselves to pin the blame on you?'

'Or someone else could have,' Oliver said under his breath.

Bones barked. 'Shh, boy,' I said, but I took it as a reminder. 'Sorry, we don't have time to discuss, Father. There's something we need to know. Do you remember Miss Stone? Our old governess. You sacked her?'

I wondered if Father would flinch at the mention of her, but his expression gave nothing away.

'I . . . years ago,' he said, looking puzzled. 'She displayed some . . . strange behaviour. I felt dreadful, but I thought it best not to have her around the family any longer.'

'Please, sir,' Oliver said, nervously hopping from foot to foot. 'Can you tell us anything about her, where we might be able to find her?'

'Last I heard,' he started, 'she was living in Ashes Lane. That's right, I think. Whether she'd still be there, I don't know . . .'

The sounds of angry footsteps descending into the tunnel suddenly hit my ears. Oliver started tapping me on the arm with increasing urgency. 'Miss Violet . . .' he warned.

'I really don't think you should be getting involved with this,' Father said. 'You shouldn't be down here, and I think you need to cease this investigation. I don't want you getting hurt, or . . .'

'*Violet*!'

That wasn't Oliver shouting my name. I turned round slowly.

It was Mother, followed by several angry policemen.

The look on her face told me all I needed to know about precisely how much trouble I was in.

'Violet,' she repeated in a low voice. She ignored Bones, who had bounced along the stone tunnel and was trying to greet her enthusiastically. 'What on *earth* do you think you're playing at?'

'I can explain,' I said, my hands raised in the air.

'Close that hatch!' one of the constables ordered.

'I'll be back soon, Edgar,' Mother said in a shaking whisper, as Oliver reluctantly obliged and pulled the thing closed again. I watched Father's eyes while the panel slid over them – his expression clear. He was pleading with me to stay out of trouble.

'This had better be good, missy,' said one of the policemen as he marched over to us and shoved us both back towards the stairs. I noticed that he didn't address Oliver.

'I just . . . I just wanted to see my father again,' I said with a sniff. I was playing for sympathy, but a part of me knew that it was true.

The other constable glared down at us both. 'All right,' he said finally. 'Upstairs, now. And if we ever catch you young'uns pulling this sort of nonsense again, we'll throw you in one of those cells! Understand?'

'Yes, sir,' Oliver and I chorused dejectedly.

Mother's hair was a mess, her skin pale with worry. Maddy peered out from behind her, shaking an umbrella on to the floor, and she looked just as concerned. I began to feel a *little* bad. 'I'm . . . I'm so sorry, Mother. I don't really have an excuse. I wanted to investigate, and we ran into Inspector Holbrook, and it all got rather . . .'

'Out!' said the policeman, pointing up the stairs. This time, we took the hint.

We stood in the entrance hall of the police station, surrounded by bustling officers, as Mother ranted at me. 'Your father forbade you from this *investigating*, as did I,' she said. 'Will it take being arrested to stop you?' Her eyes went up to the ceiling. 'Oh Lord, how have I raised such a hooligan?'

Oliver shuffled uncomfortably. 'It was important, ma'am.' I nodded in grateful agreement.

Mother's lower lip trembled, but now I wasn't certain if it was anger or sadness. 'Not you too, Oliver. I didn't know you were mixed up in this nonsense as well.'

I had to persuade her. 'We have more leads now! If you let us do this, we could prove Father innocent! If you don't, then . . .' I let the implication hang unspoken in the air between us.

The evidence was stacked against him. He would face punishment whether he was guilty or not.

I turned to Maddy. 'Maddy, please—'

She held up her hands. 'You leave me out of this, Miss Violet! You know what your father said.'

Of course, he was still the master, even if he was locked up. I frowned.

'I had to talk to him,' I said. 'I needed to know more about the suspects . . .'

'Suspects! Leads!' Mother rolled her eyes. 'Listen to

yourself, Violet. You are not a detective, you are a *girl*! I have half a mind to lock you in your room until you're eighteen!'

Now I could feel my lower lip quavering and I bit it to stop myself. I hated it. I hated the way I was viewed as a child, and a *girl* besides, which was apparently worse.

Well, if they were going to treat me like one, I was going to behave like one.

'I'm sorry.' I began to sob. 'I just wanted to see my daddy.' I felt the tears fall from my eyes. Bones pushed his nose up against me, a look of concern on his little doggy face. I dropped down and held on to him, still crying.

I soon realised that I wasn't crying falsely. As the tears came faster, I knew it was real. I missed my father. I was scared of losing him. I wanted him to tell me the truth. Everything that I'd kept bottled up was spilling out into the world.

Mother crouched and wrapped her arms round me. 'I know,' she said in a soothing voice. 'I know.' She stroked my hair.

For a few moments we stayed there, the hustle and bustle of the police station around us melting away. I breathed in the familiar smell of my mother, a little damp from the rain, with hints of her rose-petal perfume. And the warmth of Bones, who was whining softly as if he too were crying for Father.

I stood up and wiped my eyes. 'I'm sorry,' I said again, with a sniff. 'I just want to save him.'

Mother was silent for a moment. She straightened up. 'I'm going to ask to speak with your father,' she said.

We waited outside the police station for what felt like an hour, in grim silence on a park bench, while Mother spoke to the police and Father. When she came out again, there was something different about her expression, but I couldn't put my finger on it.

Something was clearly weighing heavy on her thoughts. We were almost halfway home before she began to talk to me.

Bones pulled Oliver and Maddy on ahead while Mother and I hung back. The rain had faded to a drizzle but the sky was still iron grey.

'Violet,' she said quietly.

'I'm sorry, I—' I was waiting for another lecture. Instead, I got something entirely different.

She shushed me. 'Listen to me now. Perhaps we were wrong before.' She looked up at the sky. 'Oh Lord, forgive me for what I am about to say.'

I scrunched up my face. 'What is it?'

'Time is running out, and . . . I don't . . . I don't think the police have your father's best interests at heart. I think perhaps someone needs to investigate.' She took a deep, gulping breath. 'And I think perhaps that someone might have to be *you*.'

Chapter Twenty-Seven

'M-me?' I stammered. 'But you said . . .'

'I know what I said,' she replied. 'Desperate times, desperate measures. But please, Violet – think of your safety. Stay away from the journalists. You come home the minute you see any trouble, do you hear me? And you will tell no one.'

Then, with a quick nod, as if the conversation had never happened, she hurried away towards the others. I was left gaping in the dust.

It soon hit me that for the first time ever, my mother

was giving me my freedom. Not only that, but she had shown some trust in my capabilities.

I'd always felt as though I was bringing shame to the family whenever I did anything. It was always 'Violet, stop associating with boys! Violet, practise your embroidery! Violet, stay out of your father's business!' Mother would say those things in hushed but angry tones, red-faced, always worrying about what the neighbours would say.

Suddenly she had changed her tune. As much as I wanted to feel elated, I instead felt a deep and creeping dread. My mother hadn't mentioned our desperation lightly. This was true desperation.

I was my father's last hope. The weight of his life rested on my shoulders.

Maybe Inspector Holbrook was right, and I had just been playing at investigating. It was time to take things further, and now I had Mother's backing, it suddenly all felt too real. Was I big enough to take on this task? Was I clever enough? Was I . . . *enough*? I had always *thought* I was. But what did that matter if I couldn't prove it to the world?

As I trotted through the drizzle to catch up, Bones turned abruptly and ran back to me, tail wagging. He jumped up and started trying to lick my face. I couldn't help but laugh.

'You daft dog,' I scolded. 'At least you have faith in me.'

He barked enthusiastically.

'Come on,' I said. 'Let's catch up. We've got work to do . . .'

The next day, now with Mother's blessing, we left her and Maddy to distract Thomas as we headed for Ashes Lane.

The air was crisp, the sky crystal clear but for the smoke rising from the chimneys. I'd peered through the curtains once again to find that the streets were now blessedly free of the vulture journalists, who seemed to have become bored and given up. I supposed they would make up their own salacious nonsense whether they had talked to us or not.

We dodged fellow pedestrians, Bones swerving around their legs. Many of them gave me funny looks or whispered to each other. These people were our neighbours, but it seemed none of them had kind words to spare. *I will remember that*, I told myself. I had to ignore them and their gossip. One foot in front of the other.

'We're getting closer,' I said to Oliver as we turned the corner. 'I can feel it.'

'I hope so,' he replied. Then, after a long pause with nothing but our footfalls on the pavement, he asked: 'What would happen to us if . . . if your pa . . . if we don't free him? What would we do?'

The question made the blood freeze in my veins. Oliver was trying to be gentle, I knew, but I could hear the real words hiding underneath.

If he dies. If he goes to the scaffold.

I marched ahead harder, until Oliver was almost jogging to keep up. Bones happily trotted along beside us. He liked when things moved quickly.

I didn't want to think about it. I couldn't.

'I'm sorry! I shouldn't have asked!' Oliver shook his head. 'I just thought . . . you're so used to all this. This . . .' He waved his hand in the air. 'Death, stuff.'

'We cannot argue with death,' Father had often told me. *'It is the natural way of things.'* I knew then what to say. 'It's not his time,' I told Oliver firmly. 'Today we argue with death.'

Ashes Lane was not far from where we lived, but it was fairly rundown. It was really more of an alleyway. Crooked houses leaned over each other, windows cracked with age, wet washing dangling from lines hanging between them like rows of teeth.

A lady with grey hair peeking out from under her cap stood beating a carpet in front of us, sending up clouds of dust. The air smelled of fish from the nearby market. I half expected Bones to run off in search of it, but he stayed by our side.

'Excuse me,' I said to the carpet beater. 'Does a Miss Stone live here somewhere?' It was a shot in the dark, but I hoped she might know.

To my surprise, she fixed me with a glare, before marching back inside with her carpet and slamming the door.

'Well, that was rather rude,' I said.

'She don't know,' Oliver suggested with a shrug, 'or she just ain't telling. Now we're stuck.'

Bones seemed to have other ideas. He had started sniffing along the gutter, moving quickly. 'What is it, boy?' I asked, but he didn't look up. I thought about calling him back, but I remembered how he'd found the strange journal entry before. Perhaps he knew what we were looking for? 'We'd better follow him,' I said.

Bones trotted on down the alley, his nose pressed to the ground. About halfway down, he stopped.

We caught up with him, panting.

The house he had stopped in front of was not in a good state, even compared to the rest of the alley. In fact, it looked like it had almost burned down. The windows were black, the glass cracked and melted. The stone somehow managed to look even more smoke-stained than all the other buildings in the city.

Bones sat down on his haunches and stayed completely still. He was definitely trying to tell us something.

'Does this place ring any bells?' I asked Oliver.

He stared up at it for a moment. 'No,' he said finally, with a shake of his head. 'I don't recognise it. But it gives me the shivers.'

'Me too,' I said in a whisper. The hairs on the back of my neck were standing up. It didn't look like the *nicest* place to live, if anyone did indeed live there. The alleyway seemed to be sucking out all the sound of the surrounding area, in the same way that the cemetery did. Whilst it felt peaceful and otherworldly there, here it just felt . . . wrong.

I listened carefully, wondering if there were any ghosts around, but the silence remained. Even running a finger over the rough and blackened stone, I couldn't sense anything. The place felt empty and loveless.

'What do we do?' Oliver asked.

I stood in silent debate with myself. *Knock on the door? What else could we do? Break in?* I looked down at Bones, wondering if he could perhaps find us a sneaky way to enter, but he still wasn't moving. He began to growl quietly.

'I think . . .' I started, hoping my mind would fill in the right course of action.

But I was interrupted by the sight of a face at the blackened window.

A face I had seen before. A face I had seen peering in our very windows at home.

The Black Widow. Miss Stone.

I pulled Oliver back and we flattened ourselves into the next doorway, Bones pressed between us. I hardly dared to breathe. There was a creak of door hinges, and Miss Stone suddenly emerged into the alley.

But to my immense relief, she turned away from us, and hurried in the opposite direction. For a few more moments, we stayed as still as statues, but she had soon slipped out into the street on the other side – and we were once again alone in the ominous alleyway. Bones peered out and then trotted over to the burnt house.

'Where's she going in a hurry?' Oliver asked.

'Never mind that,' I said. 'Look.'

I was watching Bones. He had gone up to her peeling and cracked door and was sniffing around it. And then, with a gentle paw, he pushed it open.

'She didn't lock the door,' Oliver said, as the realisation dawned on him. He turned to me, and must have seen the expression on my face. 'No. No, miss, we can't!'

'We have to,' I said, the decision instantly made in my mind. 'We're going inside.'

Chapter Twenty-Eight

We stepped into the burnt-out house, and all was quiet and dark. Bones hesitated on the threshold, but he was soon cautiously trotting inside, nose to the ground.

I tried to take the whole place in. The room we were in seemed to be the majority of the house. The walls were blackened and crumbling, the smell of old smoke permeating the place. What I presumed was a mirror hung on one wall to the left of us, covered with a drape as if the household were in mourning. The skeletal remains of a staircase went up to the next floor, splintered wood hanging down, unusable.

There was the hearth, a few sad embers dying in its belly, and a coal scuttle beside it. There were two threadbare chairs, and a cracked washbasin. A door at the back was open, looking like it led to another small room and presumably the outside.

'More creepy in here than it was out there,' Oliver whispered, rubbing his arms. 'Don't know how anyone could stand to stay for more than five minutes. Are you sure nobody died here, miss?'

Concentrating hard, I closed my eyes and put my hand against the wall. 'I don't feel a thing,' I told him truthfully. 'No echoes, no ripples. Just silence.'

It looked to me as if the Black Widow had just found this house and moved in. The fire must have been long ago – gutting the place, but leaving the stone walls and the dwelling either side still standing. I supposed she could have lived there before the fire, but it was hard to tell either way.

Bones whined, and I saw he had found something underneath the destroyed staircase. It was a mat on the floor, heaped with old blankets. I peered down at it curiously. 'What's this?'

Oliver came over to me, treading carefully as if the

place might fall down around our ears at any moment. 'Her bed, I reckon.'

'Oh.' A feeling of sadness and embarrassment curled inside me. This was very different from the world I came from, but perhaps not so different from Oliver's.

But he didn't seem to notice my reaction. 'Come on,' he said. 'If we have to be in here, we'd better get on with looking before she comes back. She could be here any minute.'

'You're right,' I said, trying not to think about it. 'I'll take this room, you take the next.'

'Right you are, miss,' Oliver said nervously as he followed Bones next door.

I crossed to the other side of the room, where it seemed the Black Widow had been sitting by the fire. A chipped cup lay on the table, with nothing inside it. I turned to look at the mantelpiece – on which perched a couple of faded photographs, without frames.

One was unmistakably of Miss Stone, a good deal younger than she was now, sternly posed with a group of people outside a grand house. Perhaps it was one of her earlier jobs. I examined it, but there was nothing else of note.

The other, though, was different. It was of a young pale-haired girl, perhaps Thomas's age or younger. The picture was blurred as she was (much like Thomas) apparently not very good at sitting still. I picked this one up too, and there was writing on the back. *Emily Stone, aged four and a half.*

It was the Black Widow as a young child. I wondered who her family were, what had happened to her parents. I replaced the picture carefully, and then I noticed something odd about the coal scuttle. It wasn't filled with coal or firewood, but instead with old papers and torn books. I knelt down and pulled a few out – there were bills, flyers, ragged newspapers that looked like they'd been picked up off the street. Perhaps this was all she had to burn for warmth.

But some of the papers underneath looked more personal, and Miss Stone's name on them caught my eye. There were two payslips labelled with Rookwood School – I hadn't heard of it, but the dates were after she had worked for us. Only two, though, so she hadn't lasted long there either. Rifling through, I found another payslip, dated after that – it read:

HAWTHORNE'S PAPER MILL

and it had been stamped

DISCHARGED DUE TO INJURY.

Another job lost. Could that be how she had received her scar?

'Miss Violet!'

I jumped up, but it was only Oliver from the other room. 'Come and look at this,' he said, beckoning.

I followed him back there, closing the adjoining door behind me. There was more old and battered furniture that looked as though it had been found in a rubbish dump – a three-legged table pocked with knife marks, a chest of drawers that Oliver stood beside and an open wonky bureau that Bones was sniffing around. To the right was an iron range with a rusty pot and kettle. It didn't look like it had been used for a while – the whole surround was thick with black dust and ash. A few tin cans lay discarded on the floor.

Oliver followed my gaze. 'Not much to eat. She probably has to beg, borrow or steal. Maybe that's where she's gone. Market day today.'

The sadness caught up with me again – this poor woman had next to nothing. I had to remind myself that we were on the trail of a possible murderer, not least one who could walk through the door any minute.

'What have you found?' I asked.

He pointed into the top drawer that he had pulled open. It was almost empty, save for a pair of carefully laid-out floral lace gloves.

With one glove that had a section torn off at the bottom. As if it had been torn off, say, by a loose nail in a filing cabinet at an undertaker's.

I gasped. 'Oliver! This is exactly what we're looking for! So she *could* have stolen the file—'

Just as I was about to examine them more closely, Bones suddenly barked. This time, we both jumped.

I turned. 'What is it, boy?' I hissed. 'Is she coming back?' But he was standing up at the bureau. With a swift paw, he knocked down a deep red notebook. 'No!' I cried.

He caught it in his mouth and shook it as if it were a rabbit, the loose binding spilling pages out. Oliver quickly scrambled to try and pick them up.

'Bad dog!' I chastised Bones. 'Bad . . .'

Bones had gone still and quiet, the book still clasped in his jaws. And then I heard the creak of the front door.

'Oh no,' I breathed.

'Run!' said Oliver, and he flung open the back door and raced across the overgrown yard, the papers still clutched in his hand. I turned, and saw Bones drop the notebook and shoot after him, both of them leaping the broken fence at the same time.

My heart pounded in my chest. The Black Widow was merely feet away – I could hear her moving about the house. She couldn't know we'd been there! I quickly picked up the red notebook from the floor and put it back on the desk. The footsteps were getting closer.

Wait – the drawer! It was still wide open. I pushed it back in, wincing and gritting my teeth as I willed it not to creak. Then I turned and hurled myself towards the back door, swinging it shut behind me as I went through into the chilly air. I could have sworn I heard the door to the kitchen open as I did so.

I stood, shaking, in a tangle of crushed weeds and thorns. There was no sign of Oliver and Bones.

I took a deep breath, and went to jump the fence – and my skirt caught.

'No, no, no,' I muttered, tugging at it in desperation.

Was the Black Widow inside? Had she noticed the door closing? Spotted that we'd been in there, touching her things? This was *not* the time to be stuck.

Looking up at the house frantically, I could've sworn that there in the barely transparent window were those cold eyes under black lace, staring back.

With a whispered prayer I kicked hard at the fence with a well-placed boot. There was a cracking and tearing noise as the battered wood relinquished the bottom of my skirt.

I turned, and ran as fast as my legs could carry me.

Chapter Twenty-Nine

I ran all the way home, the wind streaming through my hair. There was no sign of Bones or Oliver.

I found Mother in front of the fire in the parlour, stitching a pair of Thomas's trousers that he'd filled with holes (how that boy managed to destroy so many of his clothes, I could never work out). She was still trying to distract herself, I knew. 'Are you all right?' she asked me as I hurried in, panting.

'S-sorry,' I gasped. 'I'm perfectly all right. But . . .' I took a gasping breath. 'I've lost Oliver and Bones.'

Mother put her needle down and stared up at me, clearly suspecting there was more that I needed to tell her. 'Well?' she asked.

'We went to find Miss Stone's house. She was seen at some of the houses of the victims and, and,' I paused for breath, 'talking to the servants. I thought she might be able to help us.' I sat down heavily on the nearest chair. I wasn't sure what Mother would think of us breaking and entering someone's house, even if there was no actual breaking and if the someone was a murder suspect. So I tried to brush that fact under the rug. 'We didn't really find anything that could save Father,' I said sadly. 'But I did notice that her glove was torn – it was just like the fabric I found in our filing cabinet when Oliver's file was stolen.'

Mother frowned. 'Hmm. And what happened to Oliver and Bones?'

'Bones . . . um . . . ran off,' I said. 'And Oliver chased after him. I couldn't see them anywhere on the way home!'

'If there's one thing I know about that dog,' Mother replied, 'it's that he knows what he's doing. He'll be back soon, I'm sure. Oliver has the sense to come home before dark too.'

'Hmmph.' I didn't think Mother would say the same for me. And I didn't know how she could not be worried about them when there was a murderer on the loose!

Instead of any further concern, she simply sighed and stared into the fire. 'So you didn't find anything out? Anything that could . . . help? I don't know if a torn glove can help us that much on its own. She could have torn it anywhere.'

It was back again – the unspoken implication that Father's impending doom hung over all our words. A dark undercurrent that threatened to pull us into the depths of despair.

I rested my hand on her shoulder. 'I'm sorry,' was all I could say. I felt sure that the torn glove was a clue, that it meant Miss Stone had been the one going through the files. Mother was right, though, that even if I could prove that for certain (and how could I, without the glove?) it wouldn't prove she was a murderer.

Mother rose from the chair. 'Find out what you can, then. I'm going to check on Thomas. He's doing his arithmetic upstairs. Let me know when Oliver and Bones are home.' With that, she left the parlour, carrying the half-mended trousers with her.

I clenched my fists and followed her out into the hall, where I noticed Maddy in the shop, dusting the desk. I hurried in. 'Maddy! Have you seen Oliver? Or Bones?'

She shook her head. 'No, miss. I—'

There was a knock at the door. Instinctively, I ran to get it, thinking it could be them returning home.

'No!' Maddy shouted, and I thought she was thinking of the journalists, but it was too late. I had already unlocked the door and was pulling it open.

But it wasn't journalists. It was a man, holding his hat against his chest, the street quiet behind him. 'Oh, hello,' he said, and I could already detect the sadness in his voice. 'Are you open?'

I was tempted to point out the large **CLOSED** sign that had been pasted over the door, but the man seemed upset. If he was looking for an undertaker, that was to be expected. 'No,' I said. 'I'm very sorry. Haven't you heard about my father?'

The man's brow knitted as he stared up at the sign above the shop. 'Mr Veil?'

'Yes, he's . . . um . . .' I was about to tell the truth, and then thought better of it. 'Very sick at the moment, I'm afraid.'

'Oh, I'm sorry,' the man said. 'I'll go elsewhere.' He turned away.

'Try Flourish and Co.,' I said, wincing at having to send someone to our competitors.

How long would this have to go on for? Our business

was really starting to suffer. If Father never came back, and nobody was going to let me take over, we wouldn't be able to afford food. At least our wood for the fire came from the trees out in the cemetery, but if 'not freezing to death' was the best-case scenario . . . Well, things were not looking good.

'Really, Miss Violet,' Maddy chastised me. 'You shouldn't be opening the door. You don't know who could be out there. That newspaper lot have been snooping again.'

I ignored her reprimand. 'I thought it could be Oliver and Bones! Bones ran off and Oliver chased after him.'

'I'm sure they'll be back soon,' Maddy said, continuing her dusting. 'Perhaps you could do some piano practice while they're gone, miss.'

I gaped at her. 'Maddy, there's a murderer on the loose and Father's in jail! This is not the time for piano practice!'

She barely flinched at my outburst. 'It'll keep your mind occupied.'

Anger boiled up inside me. It hadn't escaped my notice that I was expected to play pretty tunes while Thomas learned his sums. Perhaps normally I would put up with that, but not when my friend and my dog could be in danger. Without another word to Maddy, I stomped through the house, grabbed my coat and went back outside.

I marched out of the gate and into the cemetery. It seemed as good a place to look as any. I was sure Bones would know his way home, but he knew the cemetery especially well.

It was growing dark and cold, so I picked up a brisk pace. I waved at Alfred, who was enjoying a flask of tea on one of the benches, and continued up the path.

'Bones!' I called out.

A passing mourner looked at me, horrified.

'It's my dog's name,' I explained, but she simply glowered at me and carried on walking. 'Oliver! Bones!' I tried again. 'Here, boy!'

It was as I crested the top of the hill that I heard a bark from up ahead.

'Bones!' I called again, only to have him barrel out of the trees towards me and nearly knock me over, trying desperately to lick my face. 'There you are!'

'Miss Violet!' I heard Oliver's voice, sounding a little weak and out of breath. Bones led me over to him. He was sitting in the middle of three panes of glass that were set into a stone base, surrounded by a low railing.

'You're sitting on the Hamiltons,' I told him.

'What?' He scrambled up, and I noticed he was clutching some pieces of paper.

'The Hamiltons. This is their family vault. They thought

it was too dark, so they added these to let the light in.' I tapped the glass windows with my foot. Their mausoleum was set into the hillside, so up here you were on the top, but the walls ran down the path, and lower down there was a heavy door so you could walk straight in – if it were unlocked.

There were distant whispers on the wind – the Hamiltons were all terrible gossips, and I could tell they were discussing the arrival of myself and this strange boy. Then, remembering the matter at hand, I added: 'Where have you been? What are those pages?'

'I was chasing the dog. He's far too fast for me,' Oliver replied as Bones wagged his tail happily, 'but I realised he was heading back here, an' he seemed to slow down once we were well away from the house an' that woman . . .' He held out the pages to me. 'I can't tell you what they say, miss. It's all squiggles to me.'

I reached out to take them, realising just how freezing my hands were without my gloves. They were starting to turn blue, and Oliver's fingertips were just as icy as they brushed against mine. But there was one other thing I noticed as soon as I held the paper in front of my eyes.

'Are these the pages Bones tore from her notebook?' I said with a gasp.

Oliver brushed the dirt from his legs. 'Yeah, why?'

'This is the same handwriting that was on the pieces of paper I found at the funeral.'

I looked down at the page, and there was one word that immediately stood out to me.

Revenge.

CHAPTER THIRTY

Oliver and I sat down on the chilly glass panels of the Hamiltons' tomb.

'Look at the date on this one!' I exclaimed, pointing to the paragraph I'd noticed. 'This is around when you were attacked!'

Oliver's skin paled under his messy blond hair. 'What does it say?

Week of 21st September

I read about Karma today. Retribution. I question if I am doing the right thing. Perhaps the universe should act alone, and I am upsetting its balance.

I stole aboard the Necropolis Train for three stops. It's better that way. I don't like to be seen. If I'm not seen, it is as though I don't exist. A ghost in the night. My black clothes render me yet more invisible to other mourners. I am in mourning for the life I lost.

They say that revenge is a dish best served cold.

And there they are correct.

The colder the better.

I shuddered. Whatever this meant, it didn't sound good at all. I felt as though the cold words had turned the air around us even more frosty. And it wasn't the ghosts of the Hamiltons, who I could tell were intrigued by our presence.

'The Necropolis train?' Oliver asked.

'Yes – it's the railway of the dead. It takes coffins and mourners to the big new cemetery outside the city. She must have been up to something, travelling on there.'

'Sounds like it,' Oliver replied with a grimace.

I continued reading.

Alas, I was seen. He was there before me.
He must have been waiting in the shadows by the river.
He could have run for the police. I don't trust them ~
especially not Inspector Holbrook. He's crooked
and a liar. What was I to do? I picked up . . .

I looked up at Oliver's face. 'That's all it says,' I said, with some disappointment. 'It's torn off below there.'

'Who's she talking about?' he asked, his voice low and desperate. 'Who saw her? Doing what? What did she pick up?'

'She mentions the police, and Inspector Holbrook by name, calling him crooked,' I said. 'Perhaps he caught her doing something. Or she caught him?' The whole thing sounded very fishy indeed. Sneaking onto the Necropolis train? Acting out retribution? These didn't sound like the activities of an innocent former governess.

Bones got to his feet and started stalking around in the grass. I wondered if he was trying to tell us something, but then he picked up a stick and happily tossed it in the air. There was a faint shimmer beside him – I had a sense that the Hamiltons were joining in.

Oliver smiled at the dog, then looked back at me, his expression turning sour. 'There's something I've been thinking about, miss,' he said, twirling a small stone between his fingers. 'If the inspector is pinning the blame on your pa, then . . . could he be the murderer?'

I folded the pages away carefully and put them in my pocket. 'Even if he hates my father for some reason, and he really is a bad man like Miss Stone says, I can't see what would motivate him to *kill people*. And why would he hurt you?' But something from what I had just read was clinging in my mind, refusing to let go. 'If that diary entry is from around the time you were attacked, then couldn't she be talking about *you*?'

Oliver's mouth hung open. 'Of course! If she's the murderer, maybe I was the one who saw her. That could make sense. But . . . I don't think anyone would want to murder me, miss. That they'd plan it, I mean . . .' He began tapping himself on the forehead. 'But why can't I *remember*? I don't know her. I don't recognise that house. Nothing's coming back to me.'

'It could just be your head injury. And, you wouldn't have been at her house, would you?' I said, considering the matter. 'You would have been near one of the victims. She could well have seen you, panicked, and hit you on the head to stop you running for the police! We need to jog your memory. Maybe something will come to you.'

Bones barked, though I wasn't sure if he was just joining in with my excitement or perhaps barking at the distant ghostly echoes. I really felt as though we were getting somewhere. Miss Stone and Inspector Holbrook were both deeply suspicious, and what we'd learned just proved it.

'But . . . why, miss? Why would she be doing this?' Oliver frowned and threw his stone across the tomb.

'Careful!' I snapped, making him flinch. 'Watch the glass.'

I hadn't meant to be so harsh, but even with the steps we seemed to be making, I was feeling more and more stressed with every passing minute. The clock was ticking for Father, and I needed answers that I didn't have. 'I'm sorry,' I said, tilting my head down. 'I don't know.'

'Hard times happen to all of us, don't they?' he continued. 'I was dirt poor, miss, an' I didn't go around whacking folks on the head.'

'But she writes about revenge and karma,' I said. I climbed to my feet. 'She *blames* people. For her situation.'

He appeared to ponder this as he stood up beside me, shuffling away from the glass and on to the solid stone. 'I think you're right. If she could be the murderer . . . I think we do need to jog my memory somehow.'

I nodded, deep in thought. 'Come on, we ought to be heading home. Mother will be panicking if she thinks I'm missing as well.'

'We'll get to the bottom of this, miss,' he said determinedly. 'We will.'

As Bones led us back down the path past the doorway to the mausoleum, I shielded my eyes from the setting sun. From where we stood on the hill, it was turning a fiery orange as it sank towards the horizon. The graves were bathed in amber light, the trees swaying gently in the dying breeze.

All this stillness . . . it was enough to make you forget the outside world, the murderers and strange governesses and the noose that threatened Father. It was what I loved most about the cemetery. It was on the fringe of life and death, neither quite one nor the other. Sometimes I felt that was where I was too. And Oliver, after his brush with death? Perhaps he knew how I felt.

Bones darted happily ahead with his stick, his tail wagging. On the air, the quiet laughter of the old ghosts. For a moment, the world was all right.

As I lay in my brass bed that evening, I read and re-read the pages from Miss Stone's diary. I was curled up under my quilt, still toasty warm from the bed-warmer

Maddy had left, with the fire crackling away in the hearth.

I couldn't help but think of Father, lying in a cold cell in a hammock that was no better than a sack for potatoes. There had to be something we were missing. Something that could save him.

Yet no matter how many times I read the words, I couldn't see what I needed. They began to swim in front of my eyes.

I heard a whine from the doorway.

'All right, boy,' I said to Bones. 'You can sleep on the bed again. Don't tell Mother.'

Apparently that wasn't what he wanted. He stayed in the doorway, whining and pawing at the floor.

'You want to go out?' I asked. I was met with excited wobbling and a few circular loops.

'All right.' I yawned, climbing out of bed again. It would have to be just a quick run outside, because I felt sure I was on the verge of sleep, and everyone else had already gone to bed.

Wrapped up in my coat and gloves and with Bones on a rope lead attached to his collar, I slipped out into the backyard and through the gate to the cemetery. He was pulling so hard I thought my arm might fall off.

'Argh,' I gasped, my breath making clouds in the air.

'Fine, but stay close,' I warned him as I let him off the lead. 'No running away again, do you hear?'

He stared back at me, unblinking. I followed, hands tucked under my armpits. 'Be quick about it, then!'

The night-time graveyard swam past as I tried to hurry along, feeling heavy with exhaustion. Occasionally something would swish in my ears, and I wondered if it was a greeting from a ghost or simply a falling leaf. But listening to the night's ghostly whispers wasn't at the top of my agenda. All I could think of were the words in the Black Widow's diary. *The Necropolis Train. The river. Revenge . . .*

Somewhere near the top of the path, Bones stopped and began sniffing around in the grass. *I'll just rest a moment and leave him to it*, I thought, sinking back against a broken column.

Then I realised where I was. I was beside the graves of the victims. Where the Black Widow had placed her four black roses, which were browned and wilting on the ground before me.

Interesting, I thought, but the rest of my thoughts slipped away from me. My eyelids felt so heavy. The last thing I saw was Bones looking back at me, a shadow with just a hint of shining eyes like two coins in the darkness.

I awoke.

The ground felt strange, spiky. A familiar smell filled the air. I was on a bed of pine needles. I sat up, and saw a graveyard. At first I thought it was still our graveyard, but I soon realised that the light was wrong – it was bright and white and it was shining through the trees in pinpricks. I felt the dry pine needles between my bare toes. The sun was so warm.

I realised I was inside the ruins of a church. Only two walls remained, the rest had crumbled away. Trees and creeping plants had grown up where the roof had once been. An alcove bore a faded, cracked painting of the Virgin Mary, her eyes raised skywards. The noise of rushing water came from somewhere nearby.

I turned to see a river, a little way away. It looked cold and dark, and I felt afraid to go near it.

'Bones?' I called out, and suddenly he was behind me, looking up at my face with his friendly eyes. He barked a greeting.

We were alone. Just Bones and me, and the ruins, and the river.

But suddenly – there were four figures hovering nearby. They were somehow see-through and solid at the same time. They wore top hats and well-tailored suits, and they were all pointing at me, talking amongst themselves in voices I couldn't understand.

I stepped forward, crunching through the fallen needles.

Bones began to growl, but the figures melted away like snow as I closed in on them.

As I drew nearer to the black water of the river, something huge bobbed to the surface.

I recognised it well. It was a coffin.

Three more coffins appeared, rising from the bottom of the river. Then they floated there ominously, as if waiting for me to join them.

And in the distance, I heard the distinctive whistle of a train.

I woke with a gasp, startling Bones, who had apparently lain down at my feet in the frosty grass. He jumped straight into a defensive pose.

I stared up at him, the piercing whistle of the train ringing over and over again in my ears.

'I know what we have to do!' I whispered.

CHAPTER THIRTY-ONE

At seven in the morning on the dot, I was up and dressed. My mind was racing, and there was no way I could sleep any longer. After quickly running down to grab the city map and scribbling a few notes, I hurried upstairs to the attic and knocked on Oliver's door, Bones panting beside me. Maddy peered out of her own room, where she was making her bed.

'What are you up to, Miss Violet?' she asked suspiciously.

'No time to explain!' I said, hammering on the door

again. Oliver pulled it open, and I nearly knocked on his face.

'What's going on?' he asked, rubbing his eyes.

'I know where we have to look!' I told him. 'It might jog your memory.'

Now his sleepy eyes went wide. 'Oh,' he said. 'I'll be down in five minutes.'

I hurried down the stairs to the landing below.

'Violet!' Mother called from her bedroom. 'You sound like a herd of elephants!'

'Sorry!' I shouted back. 'Important business!'

Thomas was sitting on his bedroom floor in his striped pyjamas, playing with his wooden train set. 'You're so noisy,' he said.

I quickly darted into the room. 'Thomas,' I said. 'Oliver and I need to go out. Distract Mother for me, will you?'

'Whyyyy?' he moaned, as Bones sniffed the carpet around him in search of crumbs. Small boys seemed to attract them.

'I think I've made a crucial discovery,' I said. My little brother looked at me blankly. 'You were right, Father is in a spot of trouble. But I've found something that could save him. Get him home to us.'

'Oh,' said Thomas, his face suddenly lighting up. 'All right.'

'Thank you,' I said, giving him a quick kiss on the cheek.

I prayed I wasn't giving him false hope. I prayed I wasn't giving *myself* false hope. But perhaps false hope was better than no hope.

I ran down to the kitchen and quickly made some bread and butter, and a piece for Oliver as well. Bones whined impatiently until I gave him a bit of crust, and he snapped it up.

We went back to the hallway, where Oliver jumped off the last two stairs. 'Ready!' he said. 'Let's go!' I was surprised by his eagerness.

'You've changed your tune,' I told him.

He tweaked his cap self-consciously in the mirror. 'I want to remember, miss. Not knowing is worse than knowing, isn't it?'

I knew what he meant. Not knowing Father's fate was driving me mad. If I had certainty either way – well, one of the options was still much worse, but at least I would be able to come to terms with it. 'You're right,' I said.

We went out the front way, through the shop, once I had checked that the coast was clear of reporters.

'So where are we going?' he asked.

Bones, of course, seemed to know the way already, and was striding on in front of us. I was wrestling with the map again, but I had a rough idea of where we were headed.

'I had this most peculiar dream about a river. It's helped me to put things together,' I told him. Whether or not the dream had been some supernatural message or simply my own mind reminding me of what I'd read, I couldn't be sure – but either way I felt confident. 'Miss Stone wrote in her diary that she stole aboard the Necropolis train for three stops, and that she went down by the river.'

'Hmm,' said Oliver, staring at the map as it flapped and tried to fold in on itself in the breeze. 'That could be anywhere, couldn't it? The river goes all the way through the city.'

'Yes,' I said, 'but we can safely presume that Miss Stone got on board the train at the nearest stop to where she lives.' I pointed to the crumbling alley on the map, which I'd marked in pencil. 'There are only three places it stops, and one happens to be nearby.' I tapped the station with my finger. 'And the third stop would be over here.' I tapped another station, this time down by the river. 'This is the main station. They put it near the river so that the coffins could be easily transported there. Father told me about it.'

'Maybe he told her too,' said Oliver, his face crinkling in thought.

'Hmm, perhaps,' I said. 'Or she could have been on it for a funeral. Anyway, the station is in Havisham, right next to Sadler's Croft where the victims were found. It has to be a clue.'

I folded the map away, which was easier said than done. I could see Bones again, still happily trotting, occasionally pausing to sniff a leaf or unmentionable things in the gutter. I often wondered what went on in that dog's mind.

'So what are we going to do?' Oliver asked.

'Simple,' I told him. 'We're going to catch the Necropolis train.'

The station was on the end of a row of large red-brick buildings, on a bustling street. It was a thin building, but still loomed above us from the ground below. Columns and arches stretched over the huge sign that simply read

NECROPOLIS

'I can't believe I never noticed this place before,' said Oliver, staring up at it. Bones was sniffing the entrance suspiciously as he padded around.

I shrugged. 'People don't tend to pay attention to the business of death until they need to. I'd have thought you might have noticed all of the black attire, though.' I pointed to the queue of people that snaked its way out of the wrought-iron gates.

'A lot of people wear black,' Oliver said sheepishly.

I supposed he had a point. Not least since our entire family did.

I led him and Bones over to an alcove so that we wouldn't be overheard. 'We're going to have to sneak on.'

'What?' Both Oliver and Bones looked at me as if I were mad. 'But, miss—'

'Violet,' I said for the millionth time, more out of habit than anything else. 'We don't have a choice. I don't have the fare. And if Miss Stone managed it, I'm sure we can.'

'She's one lady,' he insisted. 'We're a boy, a girl and a dog. It ain't possible.'

I raised an eyebrow at him. 'You underestimate me. What happened to playing Jack Danger? Come on.'

The queue had begun moving. We joined it, and I formulated a plan as we neared the ticket office.

Oliver shuffled nervously. 'I don't know if Jack Danger would do this . . .'

'You made him up,' I told him. 'He can do whatever he likes.'

He seemed to consider this, and then stood up a bit straighter. 'Righto,' he said.

As we got closer, I began pulling strands of my hair out to look messier. I took my handkerchief and began surreptitiously poking myself in the eyes while thinking about the saddest things I could possibly imagine. A few tears would be needed. Unprompted, my mind suddenly thought of Father's situation. I quickly had some real tears.

'Try to look upset,' I whispered to Oliver with a sniff as I batted my genuine sadness aside and focused on the task at hand. 'Bones, stay right by me.' As a black dog, he was rather hard to see when he was up against my many black skirts.

A gruff-looking ticket clerk stood in a window at the front of the station. 'You with the Barnes funeral?' he asked, waving to the people just ahead of us. 'Tickets?'

'Yes, please,' I started, and then burst into a flood of tears. 'It's my . . . my . . .'

The man's face softened a little. 'Your grandma?'

Oliver patted me on the shoulder. 'Our lovely grandma. She was such a dear. And so . . .'

I jabbed him, hoping he would get the message to stop making up unnecessary details.

' . . . old,' he finished.

I blew my nose, and threw in a wail for good measure. The actual Barnes family had already moved on ahead of us, thank goodness. I didn't want them to witness this ridiculous charade. But we had to get on that train – it was the only way with our lack of money.

I began patting my pockets frantically. 'Our tickets! I . . . I . . . Jack, have you got them?'

Oliver caught on and began searching his own person. 'Swear I just had them . . .'

A group of black-clad mourners just behind us were beginning to look impatient. The ticket clerk gave a heavy sigh. 'On with you,' he said, waving us towards the entrance. 'Sorry for your loss.'

'Oh, *thank you*, sir, this would mean so much to Grandma, you can't imagine . . .'

I shuffled away, still sniffing, Oliver's arm round my shoulders and Bones skulking along beside me.

The entrance was decorated with tastefully arranged tiles in white and terracotta. They flowed along a corridor, lit with gas lamps, that led us to the platform. I had to hide a bit of a grin with my handkerchief.

'I can't believe we got away with that,' Oliver whispered, dropping his arm.

'Shush!' I said. 'We need to keep looking sad! Let's not upset anyone . . .'

We followed the smell of smoke to the platform, where an enormous black steam engine stood waiting. Following it were carriages of black and gold, each labelled with the family name for each funeral.

Bones immediately went towards one of the carriages without windows.

'Good thinking, boy,' I whispered. I turned to Oliver.

'We'll be spotted in a second if we get into a funeral carriage. We're going to have to get in one of these.'

'What are they for?' Oliver asked, looking up nervously at the painted wood where the windows should be.

'Coffins,' I said.

The Necropolis train only went to the cemetery before returning to the city. That meant we were in for something of a long wait. Which wouldn't have been too bad had we not been crammed in a dark train carriage as it rattled along, hiding behind a pile of coffins.

Oliver looked distinctly uncomfortable, and to be honest I couldn't blame him. 'It ain't just the coffins, and the whole thing . . . that happened to me. It's . . .' He waved at the coffins. 'The dead, miss. What if they're bothered by us doing this?'

'*The dead know nothing*, it says in the Bible,' I said, absent-mindedly stroking Bones who was curled up on the dusty floor beside me. 'Well, perhaps that's not quite true,' I said, thinking of what I'd sensed over the years, 'but they're probably not too concerned. In fact they might thank us. If we can stop the murderer, they'll have more space. All the cemeteries are getting overcrowded, you know. That's why they built this railway to the Necropolis. The City of the Dead.'

Oliver seemed to consider that for a moment. 'They may know nothing, but you certainly seem to know a lot about them.'

'Ha!' I said. At least Oliver recognised what I'd learned, even if no one else did.

'Can't you hear the ghosts, miss?' he asked. 'You could ask them if they mind, couldn't you?'

I closed my eyes and reached out with my thoughts, but all I could feel was a sense of . . . peace. 'It's quiet,' I told him. 'They're not long dead. That's usually the way of things. Still adjusting.'

We sat in silence a short while. The darkness and the endless rumbling, punctuated only by occasional blasts of the train whistle, were letting my mind fill up with unwanted things. Father. Miss Stone. Inspector Holbrook. The murderer. The dead. What did it all mean?

I looked up at Oliver, just able to see his outline and the peak of his cap. 'Perhaps it's best if we don't think of the rest of the quotation.'

'What's that?' he asked.

'*The living know that they will die*,' I said.

CHAPTER THIRTY-TWO

A few hours seemed like an eternity on the railway of the dead. Eventually we heard a whistle and the guard calling out: 'Necropolis Main Station! End of the line!'

'Come on, we have to be quick, before anyone sees!' I said to Oliver. We heaved open the door and Bones jumped out and raced on ahead. We jumped out on to the platform too, and quickly mingled with the returning funeral-goers. I covered my face with my handkerchief again. It hid my identity, but it also kept the smoke from stinging my nose and eyes.

'Do you know where we're going?' Oliver asked. 'Bones seems to.'

'I'm not certain if he really knows or if he just runs in whatever direction I point him in,' I said honestly. I had my suspicions, though. That dog was a mystery, one I never knew if I would be able to solve. This mystery, on the other hand . . . 'We're near the river. I think I'll know the place when I see it. Hopefully you will too.'

We remained within the crowd. Even though I knew the funerals were sorted by First, Second and Third Class, and by religion, all I saw was the sea of black clothing and veils and tears. People comforting one another. Some even laughing and joking – the funeral was over, life carried on.

The Necropolis Main Station was even grander than the small one where we'd boarded. We took the stairs down from the platform and left through a formal entrance hall with a chandelier, then through giant gates with elaborate ironwork. An imposing building adjacent housed the railway undertakers. I stared up at it in awe. I'd forgotten how huge it was. It made our little shop look positively primitive.

'We're right by the river, miss,' Oliver said, pointing.

'Look, you can just see it through those buildings.' Even though it was freezing, the light glinted off the dark water.

But something else had caught my eye across the busy street. 'Come on,' I said to Bones and Oliver. 'I think I know where we need to go.'

The ruined church was not *exactly* like my dream, but as these things go, it was not too dissimilar.

It stood surrounded by trees, most of the walls partially collapsed, the windows empty of glass. The graveyard stood in disarray, filled with ancient stones that I couldn't read. I wondered what had happened to it. A lightning strike? Destroyed by Henry the Eighth? I couldn't be sure.

'I must have seen this place before,' I said. 'I dreamed of it, somehow. Well, it was different, but . . .'

'I don't know if I remember it, though.' Oliver shuffled, hands in his pockets. 'It does seem . . . familiar. In an odd way.'

Bones had already jumped the low wall and was sniffing through the gravestones. He seemed on the hunt for something.

I turned to look around, wondering if I could spot why Miss Stone might have come to this place. The other side of the street seemed fairly ordinary, but one thing that did stand out was a sign that read

HAVISHAM GENTLEMAN'S CLUB,

the letters picked out in gold. There were several well-painted carriages outside, and footmen waiting. The air smelled of smoke, but with a hint of expensive dinners.

Oliver saw me looking. 'What's it say, miss? Looks fancy.'

'It's a club for gentlemen,' I told him. 'Rich ones, I would say.'

'Like the folks that were killed,' he said, still staring at the place.

I snapped my fingers. 'Good thinking!'

'This seems familiar too. Wait . . .' He squinted at it, chasing the memory. 'Is it called . . . Hav . . . Havisham Club?'

'That's right,' I told him. 'Same as the borough.'

'I think I've been here,' he said. 'Yes! I have! I had this mate . . . Jimmy Tucker. He was a shoeshine boy like me. I remember . . . he told me there were rich folks round here, that there'd be good business.'

I lowered my voice. 'So you could have been here when Miss Stone was here!' I was about to suggest we go into the club and see if we could learn anything there, but Bones began barking somewhere out of sight. 'Where has he got to?'

Oliver and I hopped over the wall and waded through the overgrown grass, as I called for Bones. His bark was echoing off the ruined walls.

I ran my fingertips along some of the ancient, lichen-covered stones. The whispers in my head were quiet, old and rattling. *Inside* . . . one seemed to say, the words tickling my hair as they blew past my ear. I patted the mottled stone in thanks.

We entered through a crumbling archway. Instinctively, I looked down at the floor – wondering if the pine needles from my dream would be there. But no, the ground was littered with crunchy brown leaves instead. Ivy wound its way up the bare stone. Even with no roof, it was a little dark within thanks to the shadowy trees and the high walls. It felt hushed, secret. A place where nefarious deeds might be carried out.

Bones came barrelling over to me, his paws coated with mud. 'Yuck,' I said with a smile, batting him away.

'I think I know this place too,' Oliver said. Then, suddenly, he clutched the scar on the back of his head. 'I don't feel right, miss . . .'

Bones barked. 'Shh, boy,' I said. 'Let Oliver think.'

I took Oliver's hand gently. 'Just forget about everything else for a second, and look around. See if it comes to you.'

We stood there in silence as Oliver stared at the walls

and breathed in the air. 'I *do* remember this,' he said, the words coming out slow and heavy. 'I was . . . I was here. But it was dark.'

'What can you see?' I whispered, closing my eyes.

'Darkness, and . . . there were sounds, in here. I think I came to investigate. Maybe I thought I could sleep here for the night, you know. But I saw . . . Someone. Someone in black . . .'

Bones barked again, and I opened my eyes. He clearly seemed to be trying to get our attention. 'What is it, boy?'

He ran over to the alcove at the back of the church, and as I followed I saw why his paws were dirty. He had dug a big hole in the earth, and something metal was glinting underneath, wrapped in brown paper. I reached in and pulled it out, bits of the paper disintegrating as I peeled it apart.

I turned to Oliver, the object heavy in my hands. 'Someone with a hammer?'

His mouth dropped open. 'That's it! That's . . .' He ran over, his hands shaking, and reached for it.

'*The real murder weapon*,' I said under my breath as I handed it over. I patted Bones. 'Good boy!'

Oliver stared down at the thing. 'I definitely saw this. I saw someone being hit, I'm sure of it. Then the person in black noticed me, and . . .' His lip was quivering and he turned the hammer over in his hands, then his eyes closed again. 'I remember fear. I went cold. There wasn't time to run.' His breaths came in gasps and he clutched the back of his head.

'It's all right,' I told him gently. 'You don't need to go too far. You're not back there. You're here with me. It's safe.'

He nodded his head slowly, and I waited for him to feel calm again. Bones curled around his legs, clinging to him, reassuring.

I examined the hammer. I looked for traces of blood, but it seemed clean – aside from the dirt that covered the wrapping. The murderer had clearly wanted it hidden.

'Are you all right?' I asked Oliver when he seemed to be present again.

'It's just so strange, miss,' Oliver said eventually, a far-away look in his eye. 'To think it might've been . . . my last breath. An' all because of this.' He tossed the hammer a little way in the air with both hands, but it was heavy and he caught it with a thud.

'And if your memory is right, just because you interrupted the murderer. Can you remember who it was? Was it Miss Stone?' I asked, eager for answers.

'I can't say for sure,' he replied. 'I remember . . . a black shape in the darkness. Maybe it was a woman. It would make sense. The face was hidden, like hers usually is.'

'It all fits,' I said. We knew the Black Widow, Miss Stone, had come here – or near enough – from her journal entry. Oliver remembered witnessing something horrific here before he was knocked unconscious. And now Bones had found this hammer. 'But why would she do it?'

From all the detective stories I'd read (secretly in bed at night, as Mother and Father thought they were inappropriate reading material for a young lady), I knew you had to prove Means, Motive and Opportunity. Perhaps we could prove that Miss Stone had the Means and Opportunity, but what was her Motive? She'd had misfortunes in life, we knew, but why kill these men? Why pin it all on Father? Or were only the police responsible for that?

Even if we knew all of those answers, we had no proof.

'We need to find out why she would do this,' Oliver said, echoing my thoughts. 'We need to prove it. Or – or – have her confess.'

We needed the whole truth, and nothing but the truth. We were so close, I could feel it. 'Let's look around here and then stop by the Havisham Club. Maybe we can find some more evidence.'

We searched the ruins, and I ordered Bones to have a sniff around. There were several spots that he seemed interested in, and he would sit down and whine. But they were covered with grass and leaves, and there was nothing else to be found that I could see. If one or more of the murders had taken place there, the evidence had been cleaned up, or washed away in the rain, or hidden under the remains of autumn. Perhaps the attack Oliver had witnessed was one of the victims who had ended up in the river.

With a heavy sigh, I decided it was time to head for the Havisham Club. We left the ruins and crossed the road, dodging several fancy carriages.

'I've got the list of names,' I whispered to Oliver. 'Let's see if they were all members here. And put that away.'

Oliver looked confused for a moment. 'Oh!' he said, finally realising I meant the hammer, before concealing it behind his back.

The doorman was tall with dark curls sticking out of his cap. He was eyeing us up as soon as we neared. I climbed the steps with determination, but he stuck his hand out immediately.

'No dogs,' he said with a sneer. 'And definitely no girls.'

Bones looked at the ground sheepishly, and I glared back at the man.

'What about me?' Oliver asked. 'I'm neither of those.'

The doorman stared right down his nose at him. 'And what are you, some sort of street urchin? You're not a member, that's what matters.' He sniffed. 'Leave the premises immediately, or I shall have to call for the police.'

'No need,' said a familiar commanding voice from behind me.

My stomach filled with dread as if I'd swallowed a bucket full of stones.

'I'm already here.'

CHAPTER THIRTY-THREE

I turned to look at the looming figure of Inspector Holbrook as he ascended the steps. Bones gave a low, rumbling growl.

'Are you haunting us?'

He ignored me. 'If I recall correctly, did I not give you two a final warning?'

I looked at Oliver, whose cheeks were burning red. I wasn't sure whether it was embarrassment or defiance, but I thought it was probably a bit of both. He said nothing.

'We're not doing anything wrong,' I insisted, folding

my arms as I looked up at him. 'We're in a public place. Just talking to people.'

'Of course,' he said. 'Funny how the people you keep talking to are the same people that I wish to talk to. It's almost as if you are *investigating*.'

I gulped, but I still had some fight left. 'Well, inspector, if you would do your jobs properly . . .'

I trailed off under the intensity of his gaze.

'You would like to see me doing my job?' he said.

We nodded cautiously.

'Very well. You're under arrest for impeding my investigation.'

'No, wait!' Oliver started. Bones barked and I shushed him and pulled him behind me. My blood ran cold as I pictured us tossed in a cold cell alongside Father.

'Please,' I said, as quietly as possible. The doorman of the club rolled his eyes and turned away. 'Don't. We'll get out of your way, I promise.'

The inspector narrowed his eyebrows. 'Give me one good reason not to lock you two up.'

'We ain't done nothing,' Oliver said – but I knew that was no use. Father hadn't done anything either, and look where that had got him. We needed to try a different tactic.

'Well if you won't let us leave, perhaps you'll let us help

you,' I said, thinking on my feet. 'We know things about the murders. Let us tell you.'

He fixed his frown on me for a few moments, and I held my breath as I wondered if he was about to clap us in irons. Then his face softened, just the tiniest amount. 'Come over here a minute,' he said, gesturing across the street and away from the rude doorman. 'We'll see if you have anything of any importance. And if not, you will be going straight back to your parents. Do you understand?'

'Yes,' I said quickly.

'Don't have any— I mean, yes,' said Oliver as I elbowed him.

'And you keep that dog under control,' Inspector Holbrook added. Bones looked up at him with shining, innocent eyes.

We crossed the road, trailing after him like lost ducks. He sat down on a bench and pulled out a pipe and a book of matches. I waited for him to start speaking, but he stayed silent as he lit the pipe and a plume of the horrible smoke puffed up.

'This is my break,' he said finally. 'You talk, now. As soon as you're done, I shall be continuing my job.'

Oliver laid the heavy hammer down on the bench beside him, still wrapped in the tatty paper.

'I believe our former governess Miss Stone has a grudge

against my father.' I paused, not wanting to give too much away – I still didn't trust the inspector. 'We found a diary entry she'd written where she talked about stealing aboard the Necropolis railway to come here. Three stops away from her house, by the river.'

The inspector barely blinked. 'Show me?'

I pulled the folded diary entry from my pocket and held it in front of Inspector Holbrook's eyes.

'Hmm.'

Sensing he wasn't going to ask further questions, I continued: 'We searched the old church and found this hammer.' I waved at the parcel on the bench, and Oliver bent down to unwrap it.

The inspector merely frowned. Another plume of smoke rose from his pipe.

'I think you'll find,' I said, 'that this is the murder weapon. It must match the one you found in Father's possession. That one was planted, you see. He's been falsely accused.'

'Let's forget about that for a moment,' said the inspector, leaning forward – I frowned, not likely to forget any time soon. 'So you two found this hammer.'

'Well, Bones dug it up,' Oliver said, but his words were drowned by hoofbeats from the road. Bones looked up proudly, but the inspector ignored them both.

'But why are you trying to get into the Havisham Club?' he asked.

I glanced at Oliver, who was mouthing *no* at me. I too had realised that explaining might be seen as proof that we had indeed stolen the list of names.

Oh well, I thought. *In for a penny, in for a pound.*

'We wanted to see if the victims were members there.' I shrugged. 'It seemed the logical next step. I thought perhaps we could ask about when they were last seen at the club.'

The inspector stared down at his pipe for a moment. 'So you are telling me that you think perhaps the victims were all members of this club, and that the murderer was luring them from there to their doom.'

I shared a glance with Oliver. 'Perhaps, yes,' I said. Bones barked, and I noticed the inspector flinched slightly. *Ha!* Not so stoic after all.

'Let's consider this as true for a moment. Let's also say that most of the victims were found within the close vicinity.' He still didn't meet our eyes. 'How do you know for certain that it was not your father that perpetrated these crimes?'

The question stole my breath away.

'I . . . he . . .' I was floundering, and his eyes flicked up to mine immediately. He had found a loose thread in our argument and was pulling at it.

He pointed at the diary entry with his pipe. 'I have no way of verifying this. Your Aunt Gertrude could have written it for all we know. And your hammer?'

'The murder weapon,' I insisted, gripping Bones's collar tightly.

'A hammer on its own is just a hammer,' he said. 'All of this together – perhaps it adds up to something.' He rubbed a hand across his bristly chin. 'I mistook you for a foolish girl, Miss Veil, and you are clearly not – so I shall be frank with you. We have everything on your father for these murders, save for a confession – the hammer found in his possession that matches the head wounds, the files relating to the victims all missing from his records, the blackmail letter ordering him to harm the victims.'

So all of the files *were* missing as I'd suspected, not just Oliver's. 'But who sent the letter?' I asked desperately. I felt sure the answer was nobody. It was a forgery, it had to be.

The inspector just shrugged. 'We'll find them,' he said. 'Anyway, if this woman you believe is guilty were to confess, well . . .' He raised his hands in the air. 'That would change things.'

I bit my lip as I felt anger boil up under my skin. 'Don't you want to catch the real killer?' He seemed as though he barely cared that my father's life was on the line. 'What has my father ever done to you, that you would see him hanged over this?' My voice shook with desperation.

'He's a good man,' Oliver added quietly. Bones whined in agreement.

The inspector sighed. 'Look,' he said, 'your father and I have had disagreements in the past. He worked with our coroner for a few years before his father died, when he took over the running of the business entirely. We didn't see eye to eye.'

'So that's it!' I said. 'That's why you're prosecuting him!' Whether the inspector might be involved with the murders, I couldn't say, but this was a motive for his treatment of Father if nothing else.

'No, child,' he replied, cradling his pipe thoughtfully. 'The evidence is prosecuting him. Anger and hatred and jealousy do not speak the truth. Evidence does.'

'Unless the evidence was planted by someone who feels all those things!' I insisted. 'I don't understand why you believe he would do this, sir.'

'Why do you believe that he wouldn't?'

Oliver stepped forward. 'Because I came back from the dead, an' Mr Veil saved me!'

Chapter Thirty-Four

For once, Inspector Holbrook actually appeared to be shocked. The wind picked up, whipping leaves all around us as he stared in stunned silence.

'What are you talking about, boy?' he said eventually.

Oliver took a deep breath. 'My name is Oliver. I was living on the streets until I got whacked over the head, an' everyone thought I was dead. I was deep out of it, a coma, maybe. I woke up at the Veils' Undertaker's. It was like I died an' came back again.'

'Show him your scar,' I said. I was impressed with his forthrightness and bravery.

He turned round, lifting his hair to show the inspector, whose eyes narrowed.

'They took me in, sir. Mr Veil had me as his apprentice. But I couldn't remember what happened, until now. I think I witnessed one of the murders. Right here.' He pointed at the ruined church. 'I was shoeshining on this street. I think . . . I remember I heard a commotion an' came running, interrupted her. I got this for my troubles.' He rubbed the scar again.

'You're sure it was a woman?' the inspector asked, leaning forward. He laid his pipe down on the bench, forgotten. 'Could you say for certain?'

Oliver bit his lip. For a moment, I contemplated making him say yes, but I didn't think we needed more lies. We needed the truth to set Father free.

'No, sir,' he said. 'Sorry. Everything's foggy. But I swear I remember a black dress, an' lace over her eyes. I just . . . I just can't be certain.'

'Hmm.' The inspector sat back. I could almost see the cogs in his brain whirring.

'But I trust Mr Veil,' he continued. Bones pressed his nose into his palms, as if encouraging him to continue. 'I trust Violet too. You should believe her when she says her pa is innocent.'

The inspector's frown deepened, and he stood up. 'Look, children, I sympathise, I really do. I want the right man – or woman – to pay for this. And perhaps you have the right idea. But you must understand this. You are no detectives. The word of a shoeshine boy and the undertaker's daughter means nothing to the judge. In the eyes of the law, you are no one.'

I felt tears suddenly prickling my eyes at his sharp words.

'We will prove you wrong,' I said, through clenched teeth. Bones turned and began to lick at my hands as they balled into fists, but I gently pushed him away.

He shrugged. 'Perhaps you will. You two wait here, and I will have my men take you and your mutt back to the station. I have a job to do, child. And only twenty-four hours left to do it before your father goes on trial.' He reached down for his pipe and pocketed it.

'What?' I gasped. The world fell out from under me. Did Mother know about this? Why hadn't she told me that we only had twenty-four hours left to save him? Perhaps she couldn't face it. I felt sick.

The inspector looked down at me, no trace of his supposed sympathy in his cold expression. 'Your father goes on trial tomorrow,' he repeated. 'We have more than enough evidence against him. I am just tying up loose ends.'

'No,' I whispered, staring at the ground. Oliver gripped my hand and Bones curled around my legs.

'Please, sir,' Oliver begged. 'Listen to us! It's not him! He saved my life. What else can we do?'

'You can come to me with a written confession and the real murderer clapped in irons,' Inspector Holbrook said. He looked both ways and then stepped out into the street. 'Or you can accept that your father will die, and justice has been done.'

I would *not* accept it.

I brushed away furious tears as we once again sat in the back of the police carriage, Bones at my feet. It bumped and rattled over the cobbles, the wheels creaking ominously. Constable Williams sat on the bench opposite us, glaring. The inspector had been kind enough to confirm our suspicions that the victims were members of the club, but then had us unceremoniously taken away.

My father, I thought. *My intelligent, caring, wise, frustrating, bad-tempered father.* He wasn't perfect, but he was ours. He loved me. He loved Thomas and Mother. He looked death in its face every day of his life, bearing the weight of it without giving up. In less than a day he would go on trial, and then he would have to face his own death.

I hated to think about it. It made my stomach churn

and my skin sweat. This was no justice. Miss Stone was guilty, I felt sure of it, but what Inspector Holbrook was asking of us was impossible. Miss Stone had hidden every trace of evidence, even the files about the murder victims. She wasn't about to lie down and give us a . . . *a written confession.*

My eyes flicked up from the floor of the carriage, where Oliver had laid the heavy hammer, to the black wall opposite.

What if . . . what if she had already written a confession? Inside a certain tattered deep red notebook?

My heart began to race. Bones's ears twitched and he looked up at me.

What if we had a dog with an incredible nose who could steal it?

What if we could lure her out? Somewhere she wouldn't have the upper hand?

What if my father doesn't have to die?

Oliver was sombre and quiet after we were booted out at the police station. Constable Williams had simply ordered us to go home, the only words he had spoken to us, followed by 'go away'. I think I had preferred catching the Necropolis train with the dead. They were better company.

Bones, on the other hand, was walking with a spring

in his step. I think he could sense something different about me. The spark of hope was kindling once again in my chest.

The chill wind blew in our faces and whipped at my skirts. A discarded newspaper fluttered past in the gutter.

MURDER TRIAL BEGINS TOMORROW
ALL WILL BE OVER FOR UNDERTAKER
ACCUSED OF SENDING VICTIMS TO
EARLY GRAVES

I gritted my teeth.

Oliver must have seen my expression.

'I'm sorry, miss,' he said.

'No,' I replied, as we walked through a group of men in suits who were hurrying to get home. The clouds were grey and it felt like a storm was brewing. Oliver looked back at me, confused. 'No, I don't think it will be over.'

'Do you know something I don't?'

'I have an idea,' I said. 'Maybe. Perhaps it's lunacy. But it could work. If we . . . if we even have time.' I swallowed nervously.

Bones started circling me, the way he did when I had a treat for him. Perhaps he thought I was on to something.

‘What is it?’ Oliver asked, his voice tinged with both excitement and fear. ‘What do we need to do?’

I looked up at the darkening clouds. There wasn’t much left of the daylight, which could be a disadvantage or . . .

Perhaps not.

‘We need to build a web, and trap the Black Widow,’ I said.

Chapter Thirty-Five

We ran home.

As I unlocked the shop door, I was met by the sight of Mother in tears.

She was sitting at Father's desk, and she lifted her head as we came in. 'Where. Have. You. Been.' Her voice rattled as though it were tired from sobbing.

Oliver and I stopped still in the entranceway. Bones, however, bolted over to her and put his nose in her lap. She pushed him away. Her eyes stayed locked on me.

'Investigating,' I said. 'Like you told me to! But Mother, listen, we have a plan—'

Maddy came hurrying in and put her arm round Mother. 'Miss Violet! You've been gone so long. We were worried sick. And then we got a telegram saying you were at the police station . . .'

'They just sent us home,' Oliver said apologetically.

Mother got to her feet, making Maddy drop her arm. 'None of this is the point! I had to force Thomas to tell me that you'd gone!'

I noticed Thomas peering round the door and fought the urge to glare at him. *Sorry*, he mouthed.

My mother's face was etched with sadness and disappointment as she shook her head at me. I could understand that she was worried, but what we'd found out was so much more important.

'We've been investigating!' I said. 'Look, it's Miss Stone, it has to be! We've spoken to Inspector Holbrook and he doesn't believe us, but all the evidence—'

'I said you could investigate,' Mother snapped back. 'I didn't say you could go running off without telling me!'

'Just like you didn't tell me that Father is being put on trial tomorrow!'

Maddy gasped.

Oliver's cheeks flushed red.

Mother went stony silent.

'Is that true?' came a small voice from the doorway. It was Thomas. 'Father's going on trial? Is he going to jail?'

'Come on, young master Thomas,' Maddy said, ushering him away with a frown towards me. 'Let's go back to the kitchen.' Bones sloped after them.

'But . . .' My little brother's protests trailed off as she pulled him down the corridor.

I turned back to Mother, my arms folded. The tables had been turned.

'I was only recently made aware,' she said in a flat tone. 'I didn't know how to tell you.'

'How about "Violet, your father will be in court tomorrow"?' I said. I was being insolent, I knew, but I couldn't stop myself. 'We don't have time for this! I'm telling you, we can save him! But we need to try this right now!'

Mother's eyes stared back at me, sunken and tired. Her brow was narrowed, her hair untidy. 'Violet,' she said. 'You need to start doing as you're told.'

To my surprise, Oliver peered out from behind my back. 'Um, you did tell her to investigate, ma'am. An' – I think she's right. We have an idea. It might save Mr Veil.'

Mother sighed while I looked at him in surprise. 'I'm

not your mother, Oliver. But you do live under my roof. I think the time for investigating is over. You said you've told your suspicions about Miss Stone to Inspector Holbrook and he did nothing. So it's over. I need both of you to be home safe.' She wiped away a tear from the corner of her eye with a black glove.

'I don't think it's over, ma'am!' Oliver said, his cheeks flushing even redder. I felt a rush of pride that he was speaking up like this, just as he had done with the inspector. I'd been expecting him to try and talk me out of it, as he always had done. 'We can catch this governess before it's too late.'

'It is too late!' Mother cried.

We both flinched. Bones barked and came running back, his nails skittering on the wooden floor. He skidded to a halt in front of me, ready to come to my defence.

My mother's chest was heaving. 'It's tomorrow, Violet. We can't stop this now. We can't. I'm sorry.'

'Mother, I—'

'No! I will have no more of this! Go to your room!' she said, her voice cracking.

My skin felt hot, my fists clenched. The air was heavy with the moment. This was a crossroads, I knew. One path was clear and easy: I could listen to my mother, do as I was told. We'd stay safe and cosy in our beds, but Father would almost certainly be sent to the scaffold. The other path: dark and thorny and tangled. It was dangerous. We would be pitting ourselves face to face against the Black Widow. But it *could* save Father.

When had I ever chosen the easy path?

'Come on, Oliver,' I snapped. 'We're leaving.'

I headed towards the back of the room, to the door that led into the hallway. Bones and Oliver trailed after me reluctantly.

Mother's nostrils flared. 'Violet Victoria Veil,' she said, in a tone of voice I'd never heard her use before. 'If you leave this house, I will not let you back in again.'

We locked eyes.

And then, without another word, I left.

I gathered my skirts, and I ran again.

This time, out of the house, out into the yard, through the gate and out into the cemetery. I was vaguely aware of Bones alongside me, of him overtaking and leaping through the stones. I could hear Oliver panting as he followed.

The wind whipped at my hair, swept the tears from my cheeks. This was no time to worry, to be sad.

'Violet! Slow down! This hammer is heavy!'

My legs stumbled and I found myself clutching a chest

tomb in a bid to stay upright. Bones circled and came back to me. My breaths rattled in my chest.

Oliver caught up with me and dropped the hammer in the grass. 'Are you all right?'

I turned to him, a realisation slowly dawning. 'You didn't call me miss,' I said.

He took his hat off and rubbed his head self-consciously. 'Sorry,' he replied.

'No! Don't apologise!' I insisted. 'Oliver, your confidence is growing. And we're going to need it. This plan is pure madness.'

He adjusted his hat again, pulling it down to stop the wind catching it. 'I think I might be mad as well, following you like this. But I think it just might work.' He shrugged.

I looked around the darkening cemetery to get my bearings. We were close to the exit, so we could head out to Ashes Lane. I prayed Mother wasn't coming after us. Perhaps she'd never forgive me for this – but I knew, somewhere deep in my heart, that it had to be done. I would never forgive *myself* if I didn't try.

'Come on,' I said. 'Let's stow the hammer away, and then we'll send Bones on his mission.'

Not long later, we stood shivering at the back of the houses in Ashes Lane, behind the fence that Oliver had jumped.

'All right,' I said, taking a deep breath. 'We just have to pray she hasn't locked her back door.'

Oliver was bouncing up and down on his toes, which probably was rather conspicuous – though he would be hard to see out of the tiny, blackened windows anyway.

I turned to Bones and pulled out the diary page. I held it down for him to sniff, which he did inquisitively. 'Remember this, boy? Can you find it again?'

Bones cocked his head to one side. I had to hope that was a yes. If Bones wasn't as intelligent as I thought, our plan could go very wrong. I tried not to think about it as I patted him on the head and scratched his ears.

'Are you ready?' I asked Oliver. The large amount of bouncing and shuffling he was doing led me to believe he was very nervous, but he clearly didn't want to let on.

He nodded and blew on his hands. 'Let's go.'

He scrambled over the fence, while I pressed myself back against the rough splintered wood and cursed my long skirts that got in the way of such things. I didn't want to risk getting stuck again. Bones circled back and took a flying leap over into the backyard.

There was a *click* in the growing darkness. Had Oliver done it? Opened the door? I bit my lip and braced myself, ready to run.

I held my breath.

A few scuffling sounds came from behind me. 'No!' someone shouted.

Oliver jumped the fence and landed with a heavy thud. 'Run!' he cried.

My legs were ahead of my mind. Skirts in hand, I began to run.

Then I heard barking and shouting, and like an arrow, Bones came flying past with something in his mouth. Was it the diary? It was too dark to say, and he too fast. Bones was a shadow racing through the streets. The air was thick with smoke from the home fires burning as people huddled indoors to keep warm.

'She's following us!' Oliver panted.

I whipped my head back. Sure enough, there was Miss Stone, feet pounding on the pavement as she pursued us and what might just be the key to saving my father's life.

CHAPTER THIRTY-SIX

Miss Stone was surprisingly fast, but we were faster.

We dodged the few people that remained in the streets. A horse reared and whinnied up ahead as Bones ducked under its legs. He was far ahead, but I knew he knew where to go. The cemetery. Home. Safety.

The wind blew and a fine mist of rain fell, making the pavement slick, but we couldn't stop. The Black Widow was behind us. She knew where we were going too.

I was counting on it.

I prayed silently that my feet would stay firm. We dodged leaves and debris and market stalls being put away. Loud shouts followed us. *Causing a scene*, as Mother would say.

It wasn't long before I saw the familiar high walls and gates of the cemetery up ahead. We skidded past the funeral chapels, past Alfred who was bent over in the shed with his back to us – no doubt about to lock up for the night. No use shouting for help there.

It was uphill, now. My breaths were ragged and gasping as we followed the path through the gravestones. There was no sign of Bones now. I could hear the footfalls of Miss Stone approaching. She was closing in.

With a desperate glance at Oliver, I whispered: 'Here!'

We stopped at the fork in the path, by the familiar tomb of the Hamiltons. Oliver dived behind a tree, and out of sight. I crouched down, breathless now.

Danger, the voices seemed to whisper with the rustling of the leaves. *She's coming* . . .

Miss Stone's footsteps slowed, and I could just make her out now – both of us wearing black as night crept in on the autumn day. I watched as she lowered her own skirts to the ground and began walking slowly, purposefully towards me. A lump stuck in my throat.

'Miss Veil,' she called from the path. 'What a surprise.'

'Enough games, Miss Stone,' I panted back. 'I know what you are!'

She tipped her head to one side. 'And what is that?'

'A murderer!' I shouted. 'You killed those four men, didn't you! And you nearly killed my friend, just because he almost ruined your game!'

She stopped and pushed the lace covering from her face. Her piercing eyes stared back at me, until finally she spoke in an ice-cold voice. 'It wasn't *a game*, Miss Veil. It was *necessary.*'

Disbelief washed over me. 'How can you say that? You killed people!'

Now she raised her hands. 'The dead feel nothing. Their lives mean nothing any longer. Do you think these men did the world good when they were alive?' She shook her head sadly. 'They were cruel. They beat their servants and their wives, who confessed everything to me. They saw no problem with turning people out on to the streets.'

A chill ran through me, but I soon realised it wasn't her words – but the ghosts around me, a frisson of their anger. The wind whipped up and my hair stood on end. I swallowed, and took a step back. 'Perhaps so, but that doesn't give you the right to decide that they should die. To decide that my *father* should die for these crimes he didn't commit! This was all about him, wasn't it?'

She frowned at me, a crack in her mask. 'You broke into my house. You stole my diary. I knew *more pages* were missing. Yet you preach your morals at me.' She sneered.

I wondered for a moment why she had said more pages, and then I remembered the first entry we had found – the one she had accidentally dropped when she was handing out the accusations. 'You said someone took the sunshine from you. You blame my father for everything, don't you? What was your sunshine?'

She carried on as if I hadn't spoken. 'The men of this world think they can treat our hearts without care. They break them and crush them.' She drove her fist into an open palm. I felt my skin crawl, seeing her cold white hands and knowing what she had done with them. 'Whether servants or lovers or –' the briefest flicker of a pause – 'daughters. I couldn't let that continue.'

I felt shivers go down my spine. This was important. She'd let her guard slip just for a moment, and suddenly I understood even more.

You knew a love like the light of the sun, as I did.

Something that my father and Miss Stone could both understand. Having a child – having a daughter.

'That photograph of a girl on your mantelpiece. It wasn't you, was it? You have a daughter. Her name is Emily Stone too.'

She stared back, silent, and I knew I was right.

'Your sunshine . . . That was her. You lost her.'

Miss Stone's hands began to tremble. 'I had to give her up,' she said, and her voice was quivering too. She spoke the words to the trees, as if I wasn't there. 'We'd have frozen, or starved . . . A rich family wanted her, and I – I – I had to. I had no choice, did I? All his fault. All his fault!'

'Is that why you were stealing things? For her?' I asked, remembering the reason for her being sacked.

For more than survival, her diary had read. *For a life.*

'I just wanted the best for her,' she said quietly, her cold eyes now staring into mine. 'For her to live as you did.'

I stared back at her, feeling the sadness swell inside me. The world had not been kind to my governess, or to her daughter. 'I'm sorry,' I said, hoping that my words wouldn't get lost in the wind. The leaves rustled overhead. 'I'm sorry about what happened to you both. I wish I could have done more to help. But what you've done is unforgivable. You were supposed to be a teacher. Supposed to care for others! You could have tried to make the world a better place, but instead you *murdered* people, Miss Stone. You left my friend for dead! He's just a boy!'

She flinched a little at that. I could see that what she'd done to Oliver had got to her. In her own twisted way, she had justified what she'd done to the rich men, to my father. But she knew Oliver was nothing but innocent.

Despite her reaction, she seemed to shake it off quickly. She clenched her trembling hands and stared back at me, furious. 'I am in the right here. I am making the world a better place. I stopped those men from hurting anyone else. It's just good luck that your father got the blame. Perhaps it will teach him a lesson too.'

'You falsely accused my father,' I insisted as I stepped back again. This time she stepped forward. 'That was no luck. You plotted all of this, you put an innocent man in jail! You need to turn yourself in!'

'I can't do that.' She took another step towards me, her feet crunching on the leaves. I braced myself, ready to run if I had to. *Danger, danger*, the voices murmured, swirling around me like the leaves on the wind. A mist seemed to rise up from nowhere, fogging the air.

Then I heard a crunch, louder than the whispers. A low growl came rumbling, and Miss Stone stopped dead.

'Bones,' I whispered. I looked down at him as he padded to my side, the deep red journal still clutched in his teeth. His lips curled into a snarl. He was warning her.

'That's mine,' she said, pointing to the journal. 'You're going to let me have it, and then I'm going to leave.'

'No!' I shouted. *No, no, no*, the voices echoed. I felt

every muscle in Bones's body tense, but he kept tight hold of the little book. He knew how important it was to us, I was sure of it.

'I'm not afraid of your dog,' Miss Stone whispered, and she was near enough to me that I could just hear her over the wind and the angry whispers of the ghosts. 'I won't die for those men, and I won't die for you.' She reached into her clothing and I saw something glint. A flash of metal. *A knife*. 'You will never be anyone. They won't let you, you see. You'll only ever be an undertaker's daughter.'

That one cut me more deeply than the knife could. It was as if she knew the fear that I carried with me always. Perhaps she was right.

My muscles locked and my chest felt tight. I should have gone home. Everything in my body was screaming at me to get away, but there was no way out now. We had to do this. I took one final step back. Bones stayed by my side, continuing his warning growl.

The Black Widow moved towards me again, taking a step over the railing that surrounded the glass-top tomb. I glanced down as my heart raced. There was another rustle from the trees beside us, louder this time. I had to keep her still.

'I don't want to hurt you, Miss Violet, but I'll stop you if you stand in my way.' She held out her arms now, at the forest of headstones around us. 'Are you not afraid of this place? This place is death. All around you.'

I stood firm. 'I have nothing to fear from the dead,' I said with confidence, as tendrils of mist that only I could see began to curl up around her. 'You do, though.'

She shook her head and sighed. 'You don't understand, child.'

Her words sparked an anger that burned through whatever was left of my fear. I felt all Father's words over the years flowing through my mind. Perhaps he had underestimated me, talked down to me. But he had loved me, and he had taught me the most important things he knew. He had taught me respect for the souls of others. He had filled me with the wisdom of life and death.

'No,' I said. 'No, *you* don't understand the power of the cemetery. You don't understand *death*. All these lives, all these hopes and dreams, you think they just fade away? To nothing? Then you're wrong.'

The whispers flowed around me through the headstones. I could feel the weight of their lives giving me strength.

'This is where we plant our memories.' I took a deep breath, my eyes still on the knife. 'An apple tree in a graveyard *doesn't* just grow bones. It grows new fruit.' I waved my hand. A shadow moved behind Miss Stone. 'Do you know what this graveyard grew?'

She tipped her head.

'*Me.*'

I turned and screamed: 'Oliver, NOW!'

Oliver raised the hammer, and brought it down on the glass beneath Miss Stone's feet with an earth-shattering *crack*.

And with a scream, she fell into the darkness.

Chapter Thirty-Seven

Oliver, Bones and I all stared down into the gaping hole. A groan floated up from below.

For a few moments, I was too stunned to say anything. I could barely breathe.

We'd done it.

We'd trapped the Black Widow.

I sank down on to the stone that topped the Hamiltons' tomb. Oliver stood clutching the hammer, staring at his hands as if he couldn't quite believe what had just happened.

'The police,' I told him. 'Go. Go!'

He dropped the hammer to the ground with a heavy thud, turned and ran.

Bones seemed to have calmed. He curled around me and dropped the red book in my lap. The ghosts, too, had gone quiet, the rising mist slinking away back down the hill. I peered at the shards of glass that remained round the edges of the hole – there was frost glittering on them that I could have sworn was not there before.

And lying on the edge, a jet-black spider brooch with a few strands of pale hair. Now that I could see it up close, I could see that the outside wasn't silver at all – just coloured metal, cracked and dirty. A fake. I left it where it was.

The full moon was climbing the sky. In the dim twilight, I picked up the diary and held the pages close to my face so that I could make out the writing. I flipped through, desperate to check that it proved what we needed it to prove. Dark words, dark deeds soon jumped out at me. Names of victims. It was all there.

I hit him. He went down easily. I knew it was the right thing to do. These masters cannot be allowed to get away with their crimes any longer.

Wutherford. A cruel man. His servants tell me whispers. They see me as a friend, a confidante. I will not fail them.

Eriksen. He will not see me coming.

Comely-Parsons. Aberforth.

. . . the hammer. I didn't mean to hurt the boy. He should not have been in the way.

Will you regret turning me away in my hour of greatest need? I lost her because of you, when all I wanted was to make her happy. Now you will lose everything because of me.

The pieces are in place. The hammer, the forged blackmail letter. His debts will be a black mark against him.

I have taken his files on the victims and burned them. It will look as though he has covered his tracks. Little do they know that I am covering mine. I fear, though, that I may have left something behind. When I came home, I noticed that my glove was torn, a piece missing.

The journalists will feast on this. An undertaker who takes lives. An anonymous tip-off will do the job.

I curled up against Bones for warmth.

'Let me out!' I heard Miss Stone's voice cry weakly from below. I peered down, and I could just see the outline of the dark figure sprawled on the floor.

'They're coming for you,' was all I said.

Then Bones and I sat together under the rising moon in the company of ghosts, and we kept watch.

It seemed like forever, but eventually I heard a commotion coming up the hill. I tried to scramble to my feet, but I felt heavy with exhaustion. Bones got up and trotted over to greet the new arrivals.

It was to my great relief that I saw flickering lights coming up the path, and that they illuminated Oliver and Mother, followed by the imposing figure of Inspector Holbrook and shiny police helmets behind him. They had also fetched Alfred on the way in. He was clutching a large iron key – the spare key to the tomb, I realised.

'Violet!' Mother looked as though she had been hysterical, blotting her eyes with a handkerchief. She hurried over and threw an old blanket round my shoulders.

I hadn't realised how cold I was until that moment. I

began to shiver uncontrollably. Bones came back to me and I wrapped my arms round him.

The police constables – the useless Pickles and Williams – stopped further down the hill, in front of the door to the tomb. I watched as Alfred went to unlock it for them.

Inspector Holbrook stood before me. 'This had better not be some kind of game, Miss Veil,' he said.

'It's not,' I said. 'You'll find all the p-proof you need in t-there.' I handed over the notebook, and he took it quickly and quietly, secreting it away into the pocket of his overcoat. I prayed that I could trust him, that he would keep the evidence safe.

Mother helped me to my feet. She seemed barely able to speak, but just clutched on to me. That was another apology I needed to make. She had been so angry and I had just seen her as standing in the way of what we had to do. 'I'm s-sorry,' I said to her, though it came out as a bit of a sob. She simply held me tighter until my shaking subsided.

Oliver came to stand beside us and held up the lamp he was holding. 'It's all right, miss,' he said. 'It's over.'

I managed to stretch my lips into a smile. I felt relieved, even a little proud of us, but we had just brushed so close to mortal danger that it was hard not to feel in shock.

Inspector Holbrook picked up the hammer as if it weighed nothing. 'Hmm,' he said.

I watched as Alfred stood back and the constables shouldered their way through the heavy wooden door into the tomb.

They emerged not long later, holding up a hobbling Miss Stone and the knife she'd been carrying. Her heavy black clothes seemed to have protected her from the breaking glass, but there were a few cuts on her skin. She said nothing, didn't even meet my eyes as they took her away.

I breathed out. They had her now.

'You should all go home,' the inspector said, turning back to us. 'We'll take this woman for questioning. Get some sleep.'

'Will you free my father?' I asked. 'He won't have to go to trial now, will he?'

The inspector looked down at me. 'We'll see,' was all he said.

Not long after, I was in bed with a fire blazing in the hearth and Mother and Maddy tucking me in.

'Don't you frighten us like that again, Miss Violet,' Maddy said. She gave me a gentle smile and then went to stoke the coals.

I was about to say I couldn't promise anything, but I

thought better of it. 'I'm sorry,' I repeated for what felt like the thousandth time.

Mother kissed my forehead. 'I'm sorry too, my darling. I should have told you about the trial.' She sighed. 'I . . . I felt as though I was drowning in all this.' Bones jumped up on the bed and laid his head in her lap. For once, she didn't push him away, but sat stroking behind his ears. 'It seems you might have thrown us a lifeline.'

'Did you know that she was stealing things?' I asked, laying my head back on my downy pillow. Everything felt so warm and cosy after the cold cemetery. 'For her daughter?'

Mother went still for a moment. 'I . . . I always thought she was a little strange, and I had noticed the odd missing item. Some of your toys and clothes, even.' She frowned. 'I presumed they were lost. If she had only asked, I could have passed some on . . .' She sighed. 'I think your father realised the truth, and he must have felt sorry for her, if I know him. All I knew was that he had seen it fit to let her go.'

I yawned. 'You didn't ask why?'

She stared down at Bones for a moment. 'No. It was his choice, as head of the household. Perhaps . . . perhaps I ought to have.'

'Goodnight, young miss,' Maddy called from the doorway. 'Stay in your bed tonight, won't you?'

'For tonight, I can promise I'm not moving,' I said. The warmth of the quilt seeped into my skin.

Mother stood up, causing Bones to reshuffle his position. 'We will go to the police station first thing in the morning and find out what's happening. I promise.' She kissed me on the forehead.

I smiled sleepily. Bones curled up next to me.

'Don't think you're not in trouble, though,' she said as she walked out of the room. 'I'll have you polishing the coffins for the next three weeks. And you can dust all the immortelles.' I thought of our vast display of porcelain flowers. That was going to take a while. 'And . . .' She paused for a minute in the doorway. 'You can darn all of Thomas's socks that get holes in from now on!'

I pouted back at her, but she just gave me a small smile and left.

I nestled into the covers and petted Bones. A few minutes later, Oliver appeared in the door, glancing around to make sure Mother wasn't looking. He leaned against the frame. 'Are you all right, mi . . .Violet?'

'I am,' I replied, appreciating that he was making the effort to say my name. 'How about you?'

He smiled at me. I noticed that his hair was sticking up and his jacket was hanging loose, but his posture was easy. He seemed more relaxed than I'd ever seen him. 'I feel . . .

lighter,' he said. 'Just knowing she's been caught. I didn't realise how much it was weighing me down being . . . being afraid all the time.' He rubbed his hand through his messy hair and exhaled deeply.

'Oh, Oliver,' I said, propping myself up on my elbows. 'You should have told me!'

He shrugged. 'I was trying not to think about it. But just knowing someone was out there who did that to me . . . it was scary. An' I didn't know why.'

'It wasn't your fault,' I told him. 'You were just in the wrong place at the wrong time. Nothing like that will ever happen to you again.'

'Not with you two here to protect me,' he said, grinning at me and Bones. The dog thwomped his tail on the bed in agreement.

I chuckled. I hoped that was true.

'Your . . . your pa's going to be all right, isn't he?'

I crossed my fingers on both hands. 'We can but hope.'

Oliver nodded a little sadly, but I think we were both feeling a lot better. Tomorrow we would really find out my father's fate. Had we done enough?

'Goodnight.'

'Goodnight.'

I lay back, stroking Bones again. 'Well done, boy,' I said. 'You're the best dog ever.' He looked up at me, with his deep dark eyes like galaxies. 'We'll give you the juiciest bone we can find, I promise.' His tail gave another sleepy swish and then he began to snore.

When I finally fell asleep, I dreamed of opening a tomb, and of doves flying out into the sky.

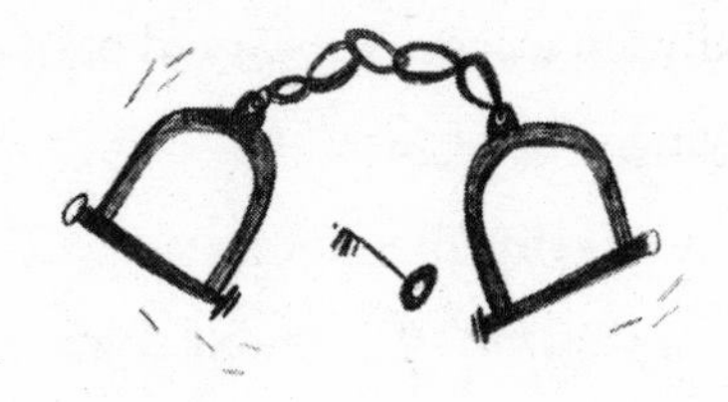

Chapter Thirty-Eight

The next day, I was up as soon as the sun rose. It was a weaker sun as the autumn days spilled into winter, but when I pulled open the curtains it still lit up the room. The place was getting dusty. I was sure Mother would put me on the duty of cleaning it as another punishment, but I didn't feel so bad about it. My world was turning again.

All of us went down to the police station, bundled up in our coats and gloves. Bones trotted along beside us.

Maddy held Thomas's hand and I trailed along beside Mother and Oliver. We were all too anxious to speak.

The station was quiet that morning, the waiting area mostly empty – with one notable exception.

'Father!' I cried.

He was standing by the door that led to the stairs, with Inspector Holbrook. Constable Pickles had him in handcuffs. There were bags under his eyes, and his face was unshaven. For one horrible, everlasting-seeming moment, I worried that we hadn't done it. That Miss Stone had escaped justice somehow, and they were taking him to the trial.

But then his blank expression cracked into a huge grin as Constable Pickles unlocked the handcuffs.

I ran over and threw myself into his arms.

'Steady, girl,' he said, putting me back down.

Thomas ran over too. 'Daddy!' he shouted as Father leaned down and put his arm round his shoulder. Bones barked and circled excitedly.

Pickles rolled his eyes. 'That blasted dog. Can we get him out of here?'

I put my hands on my hips. '*That blasted dog* helped us catch the real murderer, unlike— Mmmf!' Mother had clamped her hand over my mouth.

'What my daughter means to say,' she told them as I

wiggled away, 'is that we are relieved that justice seems to have been done. Is my husband free to leave?'

Inspector Holbrook gave the curtest of nods. He turned to Father. 'Mister Veil – you may go.'

Mother exhaled a shaky breath as she went over and took Father's hand. The happiness sparkled in his tired eyes. The two of them stepped away from us for a moment and talked in low voices. Thomas laughed and patted Bones enthusiastically while Maddy watched them with a huge grin. Pickles merely glared and walked away.

Oliver, to my surprise, came and stood next to me and drew himself up to his full height in front of Inspector Holbrook. 'Don't you owe them an apology, sir?'

The inspector's mouth dropped slightly open. Then his eyes narrowed as his jaw tightened again. 'I don't make apologies,' he said. 'I follow the law.'

'Well, the law was wrong,' I replied. 'Miss Stone was the murderer, not Father. You imprisoned the wrong person.'

He snorted. 'You have some gumption, girl, I'll tell you that. Well, yes, I can confirm that your Miss Stone has confessed after we captured her. With the written record of the murders and the real weapon, and the fact that she was wielding a knife at the scene, the case is iron clad.' Then something changed in his expression. 'Just a stroke of luck, I suppose, that she fell through that glass-topped tomb and became trapped. Along with her confession.'

I opened my mouth, but said nothing. For once, I realised the wisdom of not speaking. I glanced at Oliver, and he grinned back at me. Somehow, Inspector Holbrook's omission was the greatest compliment he could have given.

'Will that be all?' he said.

There *was* something I wanted to ask him. Something that I knew would eat away at me if I didn't say it. 'Sir . . . Miss Stone had to give up her daughter. Would you be able to find her? Tell her what's happened? Perhaps she'd like to meet her mother, even though . . . well, you know.'

The inspector scrutinised me for a moment as if I were a complicated puzzle that he didn't quite understand. 'Hmm,' he said. 'Very well then.'

With that, Inspector Holbrook raised his eyebrows, pulled his pipe out of his pocket, and excused himself to leave.

I breathed out.

Mother and Father came back over to us, Mother red-faced and beaming. Father clapped his hands together. 'We should get back. The business needs me. Violet, have any customers been in?'

I felt a rush of pride that he was asking me about

the business. 'We had to close up, Father. I'll have the word sent around that you're free – and not guilty of any crimes – as soon as possible.'

'Good girl,' he said. 'We have a reputation to rebuild. And . . .' he paused, looking a little embarrassed. 'I have debts to pay off. The blackmail may have been a forgery, but I don't want anything like this ever to happen again.'

I smiled up at him. *We can do this*, I thought. *We can make the business better than ever, together.*

'Perhaps you ought to take some rest first, Edgar,' Mother chastised.

'Nonsense,' he said with a smile. 'I need to keep busy. We must get this behind us. There's no time to waste.' I had to wonder if he would feel the same once he was home, but perhaps he really was just filled with relief at his freedom. It was as though his life had a whole new start after coming so close to ending.

'Father . . .' I asked in a low voice. 'Did you know? About Miss Stone? I mean . . . did you suspect . . .?' I didn't really know how to ask the question.

He frowned a little. 'Not really, but . . .' He turned to Mother. 'I should have told you all that was going on.' He hung his head. 'I felt sorry for her, you know. I couldn't keep a thief in the house, nor could I let anyone else hire one in good conscience, but I realised she was stealing for her daughter. I thought it kinder to keep it quiet. Perhaps I should have had more empathy, tried to improve her situation. If I had known . . .'

Maddy was watching him carefully, not saying a word. He looked up at her.

'I will not repeat my mistakes,' he said. 'You are safe with us, Maddy. You too, Oliver. We'll do our best for you.'

'Thank you, sir,' they both replied. Happiness blossomed inside me. Oliver was here to stay!

Father looked at us. 'The police said you two were responsible for catching her. Is that true?'

'Yes, Father,' I nodded sheepishly, unsure whether I was about to receive praise or a telling-off. 'Well, Bones helped.'

Father tickled Bones under the chin. 'Good boy,' he said. His eyes raised to us again. 'It seems I underestimated you, daughter.'

I fought the urge to grin and tell him that I had told him so. I had *always* told him so. Perhaps now he saw what I meant.

My father was asked to sign a few pieces of paperwork, and then we were really free to go. What I wasn't expecting was the crowd of journalists that had suddenly gathered outside the station.

'The vultures, again!' I exclaimed when I spotted them.

'How did they get here so quickly?' Bones barked a warning and I grabbed hold of his collar. There was a small sea of arms brandishing notebooks and pens, with the odd photographer amongst them.

This time, though, things were different.

'Mr Veil! Is it true that you've been cleared of all charges?'

'Mr Veil! Tempest Smith, *Weekly Bugle* – did you know the accused?'

'What can you tell us about the new suspect?'

Father raised his hands graciously as we descended the steps. 'One at a time, gentlemen. I will answer some of your questions, but then I really must get home with my family.'

A familiar journalist stepped forward. 'Briar, *Morning Times*. Reports are calling her the Black Widow. How did they catch her?'

Father turned to me. 'I think, perhaps, my daughter might be the one to answer that.'

EPILOGUE

Winter came with a sharp frost on the air, and then the snow fell. The cemetery was beautiful, draped in white, untouched.

Untouched, that is, until Bones raced out into it, leaping through the snow and barking with joy. He rummaged with his paws, spraying white flakes in all directions.

'Calm down, boy,' I said, laughing, as Oliver and I jogged along in his wake.

'Wait for me!' Thomas called after us. He was dragging

his favourite red kite behind him, the ribbon ends trailing on the ground.

Father waved out of the back door at us. He was heading out to the stableyard to meet his men for the day. Business was really picking up now – which perhaps was uncouth to say when it came to the business of death. But death went on no matter what we did. We were the ones who helped others to remember, who dealt with things so they didn't have to.

Father was allowing me to help out a little more, and Oliver was on duty most days. Father thought it wouldn't be long before we could afford to give him a small wage.

That day we had been given the morning off while Father arranged a ceremony. The snow was our reward.

Bones dashed up the hill, the snow coming up his long legs quite a way. It was deep and fluffy. A lone robin tweeted at us from one of the headstones as we made our way along the path.

I sighed with delight. 'Isn't this beautiful?'

'It's freezing,' said Oliver in a teasing tone. 'I can't feel my nose.'

I gave him a gentle jab in the shoulder. 'Don't ruin it!'

Oliver had grown in confidence and happiness in the past few weeks, slowly shedding the weight of what had happened to him.

I felt relaxed too, but I had to admit that something inside me was itching for adventure. I kept thinking of Miss Stone's words – that the world would never let me be anything other than an undertaker's daughter. All my life I had wanted to be seen as more than that, to help with the business in my own right. Even if I managed to prove to my parents that I could be an undertaker . . . would I be content with that? Or did I want something more?

I think, deep down, I already knew the answer. I was going to change how the world saw me. After all that had just happened, I was no longer sure if undertaking was for me. But solving mysteries – investigating, helping people, stopping villains – the thought thrilled me.

Violet Veil: Private Investigator. I grinned as I walked. *No: Consulting Detective.*

It was time to find my own work. Work that bridged the dead and the living, just like me. Could I do it? Would anyone support me? Only time would tell.

Oliver and I reached the top of the hill, and I swept away the snow on an old chest tomb, its edges dripping with icicles. 'Sorry, Mr Bonneville,' I said as I hopped up on to it. 'You've got the best view. I hope you don't mind.' A ghostly chuckle tickled my ears, and the cold tomb became a little warmer.

Oliver jumped up beside me, and we looked down over

the cemetery. It was blissful – untouched and white and quiet but for the gentle wind that blew the tree branches. The rows of stones laid out before us, winding down the hill to our house, and beyond that the city with its thousands of chimneys puffing smoke.

The silence was broken by Thomas whooping as he launched his kite into the air. It was a funny sight – the small boy in his best black suit, trailing a soaring bright red kite over the graves.

I ran my fingers over the words on Mr Bonneville's tomb. *That which thou sowest is not quickened except it die.* Father had told me about this one, once. It meant 'what you sow does not come to life unless it dies'. He said it meant that endings are what give life meaning.

'What do you want to do with your life, Oliver?' I asked suddenly.

He smiled and pulled out the waxed paper bag containing bread and cheese that Maddy had given us. 'I'm happy sitting here, Violet.'

'I mean in general,' I said as I watched Thomas's kite flutter in the breeze. 'Now that you have a whole life ahead of you, with no murderous women lurking in the bushes? Or at least, so we hope.'

'I don't know,' he replied. 'I suppose I'll find out.'

I smiled at him and took a piece of bread. It was still

warm from the oven. He had a point. Perhaps I didn't need to know exactly where my destiny would take me. Not yet.

I was born in the mortuary. One day, I suppose I'll end up there too.

It's what's in between that counts.

Dear reader,

I do hope you've enjoyed reading the first of Violet Veil's adventures. I wrote this book partially to help myself deal with loss. It was actually rather enlightening and empowering to live through this character that faces death on a daily basis without ever losing her sense of self or purpose. She sees it for what it is – the natural way of all things, the autumn that must come to make way for the spring. But that doesn't mean that she doesn't value life – in fact, quite the opposite. She knows that life is precious, and she'll fight to defend it and to bring justice to those who would try to take it away from anyone else.

Many people have helped me to bring Violet's world to you. Thank you to my editor Michelle Misra for believing in the book – without you it would never have seen the light of day. And to Samantha Stewart and all the team at HarperCollins *Children's Books* who have worked so hard on getting everything just right, from the text to the cover to the sales and marketing. You're all superstars.

Special thanks to Hannah Peck, whose incredible illustrations have really brought it all to life!

Thanks also to my agent Jenny Savill and all at the Andrew Nurnberg Agency for your continued support. I mentioned the idea for this story to Jenny at our very first meeting, and her enthusiasm has kept me going throughout the years.

To my Writing Group of Wonders: Bernie, Charlie, Kim, Sarah and Sue – who have spent so much of their time reading chapters of this story and offering invaluable feedback. You can thank them for suggesting that Violet needed to have a dog!

To my class at the Bath Spa MA Writing for Young People – in what seems like the distant past now, they read the very first chapter of this book after I stayed up late into the night writing it because I couldn't let the idea go.

To all those who have shared precious knowledge with me – many thanks, and I must note that any inaccuracies or wild jaunts away from the historical truth are my own. I should add that another reason for the writing of this series is my lifelong obsession with graveyards and cemeteries. They are incredible, fascinating places filled with history and nature. Two of my absolute favourites are Arnos Vale in Bristol, and Highgate in London, both in need of our support and protection. In particular, I have been to some wonderful events at Arnos Vale that have filled up my well of wisdom with all sorts of melancholy curiosities – and I must give special thanks to Kate Cherrell (of the wonderful website *Burials and Beyond*) for sharing her expertise on Victorian mourning there.

To Nightwish, as always, for reminding me to dance before the scythe.

To my husband and daughter, family and friends – my books could not happen without you all and your love (although they might happen a bit faster, it has to be said . . .)

And finally to you, the reader. Whether you've read my Scarlet and Ivy series or you're completely new – welcome. I hope you enjoyed your stay in Seven Gates. Violet, Oliver and Bones will return soon!

Sophie Cleverly